LOST CHILDHOOD

by Maria Louise Wilson

Copyright 2018, M.L. Wilson

ACKNOWLEDGMENTS

I want to thank my husband for helping me with my computer problems and my sister, Sonya, for helping me edit my story. Thanks to my friend, Claudia, for keeping faith in me, Marion for her encouragement, thank you Patricia for inspiring me to finish the book and Mr. and Mrs. Ratzburg for their input. I am also grateful to Collette for her willingness to help.

I dedicate "Lost Childhood" to my family. My children, Mark, Lisa and Philip whose helpful suggestions were appreciated. Also, I wrote this for my grandchildren, Ayden, Alec and Aria and my siblings, Sonya, Ronda, Michael and their families and my angel brother, Rickie, whom I believe is my guardian angel.

I hope they will have a better understanding of my mother's life during WWII and love and respect her even more. Margot was a beautiful, caring mother. She was a shining example of selflessness, sacrifice, love and friendship. Her children couldn't have asked for a better mother. We all agree she was the best.

TABLE OF CONTENTS

MARIA L WILSON

LITTLE ANGEL

THE END OF DESTRUCTION

GERHARD HEADS HOME

LUISE WANTS TO GO BACK TO COLOGNE

LUISE WAITS FOR GERHARD'S RETURN

THE AMERICANS ARE COMING

HEAVEN IS WAITING FOR YOU

THE BEGINNING

Fire, fire everywhere! Stop, please stop. Oh, that penetrating noise---the bombs endless deafening echoes as they fall from the sky. I can see clearly that horrid, revolting arm sticking out of the ground stretching out to grab me like a zombie without a body. It's as if it is swaying with the haunting music of the bombs. I turn to run away from the chaos, but everywhere I look, the view is the same. The severed head seems to rotate with each movement that I make watching me with a death stare that pulls the life out of me. I don't dare move in fear of being struck dead by the horror of it all. How do I get out of here? Help me someone. Then I start to run as fast as I can. I must get out. I run past the evil head and fall into the bushes. As I reached up to grab on to something to bring me up to my feet, terror filled my soul when I felt something chilling cold run down my arm. I looked up and saw I was holding the bloody dripping leg of a human being. Will this hell ever end she thought as she woke up crying again. Not as long as I have these reoccurring dreams. It's been fifty years since then and everything has changed except the dream. Is this my eternal nightmare? She whimpered as she slowly pulled herself up out of bed. It was only three in the morning, but she could not go back to sleep. She walked into the kitchen and made herself a cup of coffee. A lot of memories were swimming around in her head twisting and turning like a whirlpool.

She tried to go back in time when her memories were happy and carefree, before the horrible nightmare. Her thoughts turned to the little town called Furth im Wald at the edge of the forest in Bavaria. It is a beautiful storybook village surrounded by a little mountain called Hohen Bogen which means high arch. As a small child she would oftentimes sit on the balcony of their third floor apartment and watch the awakening sun cast the first beams of light on the majestic snow capped peaks of the mountain. It was an especially cold winter that year and the softer days of spring seemed to be hiding. She was shivering as she braided her long dark auburn hair. She had a small mole a little to the left of her nose over her mouth. Her father told her it made her look like a movie star, but she was not convinced. She thought of it as a hideous flaw on her face. She tried not to think of it as she lifted her head and stood up. Her brown eyes widened when she suddenly spied the morning's radiant glow of sunrise opening up the gray lifeless sky. "Margot," called her mother, "You must be freezing out there. Come inside and eat your breakfast. We don't want to be late for church." Margot's mother, Maria Meier, was a stern, strict woman who was taught to be neat and orderly. She always wore her long brown hair in a tidy bun and had a hardened look in her eyes. Although she had a good heart, Margot cannot remember ever seeing her laugh. She showed her love with her loyalty and devotion. However, her father, Ludwig, was her beam of light glimmering in the darkness. He was of medium built and just a little taller than Maria. He was a calm quiet man with a wonderful sense of humor. He always knew how to comfort the people around him. His brown eyes twinkled whenever he gave Margot a wink. He worked at the glass factory just outside of town. Margot's sister, Ilse, was two years older than her with golden blond hair that shimmered in the sunlight. They sometimes argued as sisters do, but most of the time they were best friends. They had a special trust that allowed them to tell their innermost secrets to each other. Margot also had a sister 10 years older named Luise. She had recently gotten married to a handsome young man named Gerhard and moved to the city of Cologne.

"Hurry children," called Maria. "Finish your breakfast. You know how I hate to be late." Maria was a good cook. She never measured anything with a measuring cup. She just poured whatever needed measuring in her hand and threw it into the bowl and mixed it into the right proportions every time. Ilse and Margot ate fast and grabbed their coats to join Ludwig and Maria.

Margot could hear the tones of the crystal clear church bells ringing in orchestral harmony on that Sunday morning as she, her mother, father and sister made their way down the steps of the apartment house. With the sun on their backs and the fresh smell of the clean mountain air, the walk to church was refreshing. All the stores and restaurants were closed, so there would be no distractions to take away the breathtaking moments of the atmosphere.

Church was usually boring, but today, Margot and Ilse walked hand-in-hand as they took their seats with the choir. They had been practicing together all week to prepare. Maria and Ludwig watched proudly as their two daughters sang with loud voices. They knew that Hitler was opposing many of the church's policies. Hitler had his own idea of religion and wanted control of all the churches such as stopping publication of the Bible and removing the crucifixes and saints from the alters and classrooms. He wanted the book he wrote himself, Mein Kampf, (my struggle) to replace the Bible and swastika to replace the cross. Although the clergy were not allowed to participate in politics, they were one of the first components of the German Resistance. The churches, catholic and protestants, were not in a position to openly oppose the Nazi State, but they caused a lot of friction. Many individuals and priests spoke out against the Nazi regime and most were killed or taken to concentration camps.

When morning service was over, Margot always stopped in front of the life size picture of Jesus and made a slight curtsy before she left. To her, he looked like he was floating in air with his glowing white robe and bare feet. His outstretched arms were an inviting form of comfort.

After church they always walked to the cemetery to clean the grave sites of their grandparents. Even in the winter the snow had to be swept off the gravestones and a prayer needed to be said. For Margot the best part was the climb up the hill where pictures of Jesus were encased in glass with each picture showing a portion of his trek to Calvary as he carried the cross. It caused her to reflect upon life and helped her to appreciate all the good things that God had given her such as her family.

During their walk home, Margot's thoughts rested on the far away business trip her father was taking in the morning. His disposition was a good asset for his job. He was the one asked to travel as far as the USA to represent the glass factory and present new innovations. Tomorrow was one of those days that would send him far from home.

"My little bluebird, why are you so quiet," asked Ludwig. "You look like you've just broken one of your wings."

"Oh father, must you leave again," replied Margot in a somber voice. "Why do you have to go all the way to America?"

"I know my job requires me to do a lot of traveling, but I'll make it up to you when I get back. We'll go to the woods and hunt for mushrooms."

"What will you bring me from America?" demanded Margot.

"I don't know yet. This will be my first trip there. It'll be a surprise to both of us," stated Ludwig.

"Don't forget about me, father," cried Ilse with a frown that looked as counterfeit as her glass ring. Her blue eyes fluttered as she slowly bowed her head toward the ground. She was distinctly jealous of her sister and father's close relationship.

"I'll have a surprise for you too, sunshine, don't fret," said Ludwig with a consoling voice. "Now let's hurry home for lunch. I have a lot to pack to get ready for my trip."

Maria made a special meal with dumplings, sauerkraut and pork. Ludwig always made the salad and lemon tea for the Sunday meal. He usually helped Maria wash the dirty dishes. Margot loved to watch her parents work together in the kitchen. It gave her a sense of security.

Morning came too quickly. Maria laid out some sliced meats and Farmer's bread on the breakfast plate. They hurriedly ate their morning meal and rushed to get dressed. "Ludwig," called Maria, "it's time to walk to the train station. We don't want to be late."

Ilse and Margot ran to the basement to retrieve Ludwig's bicycle. It will be easier to transport the luggage that way rather than carry it three miles. They placed the suitcase on the seat and pushed the bicycle down the bumpy cobblestone street. Margot skipped along side as they sang their songs. The anticipated long walk seemed much too short. "Well, here we are," said Ludwig. " Give me a big hug my little family." He held out his arms and Margot clutched his leg and held on for dear life, but to no avail. Soon the train squealed to a halt and Ludwig stepped onto the platform shouting, "I'll be back in four weeks. Don't worry." They waved goodbye and watched the train as it disappeared down the track.

Slowly, the days became longer as spring ultimately showed it's face and the melting snows allowed new growth to poke through the soft, dank ground. Ludwig returned with the promised gifts. "I have two wrapped presents. It was hard to choose which one to give to each of you so choose one," he said as he held out both hands. They each chose a gift and opened it. Ilse held up a little round red music box with pictures of snow white and images of dwarfs going by a die cast window. As it rotated, the Heigh- Ho song was playing. Ilse screamed for joy and Margot started jumping up and down when she saw her little Grey Rabbit music box. As she pulled out the small drawer on the bottom front, music played and the little rabbit started to dance.

"You better put those in your rooms before you break them," said Maria. They hugged their father and ran to their rooms with the new music boxes.

Every day Margot would pester Ludwig about going to the woods to pick mushrooms. "You promised," she repeated until her words echoed in Ludwig's ears. Her persistence finally paid off. "Okay," exclaimed Ludwig, "There may be some mushrooms ready to gather," and her father agreed to take the trip. The morning was still drab as Margot, Ludwig and Ilse reached for their sweaters neatly hung by the door. At the bottom of the stairs, Margot suddenly stopped in her path. "Why are you peeking out of the door? Go on out," said Ilse.

"No! Wait a minute," said Margot, "We can't go yet."

As Ludwig opened the door and looked out he exclaimed, "Oh, she's afraid of the chimney sweep!"

"That's just plain silly," said Ilse. "He's just a man covered with soot you scardy cat."

"All right, he's going around the corner. We can continue our journey now," said Ludwig.

"Father, why does he have to look so scary?" asked Margot.

"It's only scary in your own mind, Margot. He is really a very nice man and he offers a very needed service especially after such a cold winter. Always remember to treat every person equally even if you don't understand everything about them.

"Hurry," said Ilse as she was running ahead toward the narrow path in the woods that led to their special little mountain. "Mother will be waiting for the mushrooms to make with dinner. I'll race you to the tree with the boards nailed to it. Maybe a wild boar will come along and chase you up the tree or better yet, you can't even reach the first board. The boar will tear you to pieces before you can get away."

"Oh be quiet, father will carry me up the steps of the tree. You will be the one left behind," yelled Margot as she ran up the hill toward the top of her mystical land of wonder where the trees were giants and the animals were magical.

"Why does she have to yodel like that every time we come here? What if someone hears her? She is making a complete fool of herself," complained Ilse with her hands over her ears.

"You know how serious she becomes when she climbs toward the top of our little Hohen Bogen. After all she is only eight years old and you are ten so you should be a good example for her."

Just then Margot came running, "Do you think God heard me this time? I yodeled as loud as I could."

"It's just a tiny little mountain. God can't hear you. You're just a silly stupid goose," said Ilse.

"Whether He can or not, we have to respect her belief in it," said father. "My little Margot, you are getting much better. Soon you will be able to do the Kuckoo yodel like a pro."

"Can't you at least pick a slow melodic yodel that someone might want to listen to," added Ilse.

"I want a fast, lively one that will wake Him up in case He's asleep," answered Margot.

"Why do you have to be so silly about everything you goose. God doesn't sleep!"

"That is enough, get your baskets and let's get busy picking these mushrooms before it gets late."

"Pay attention to what you are doing," said Ilse, "Do you want to poison us! You know better than that. Don't you remember which ones to pick and which ones to leave alone." But Margot wasn't listening. She was daydreaming about her magnificent extraordinary world and about the little town she lived in. Furth im Wald is located in the Bavarian forest close to the border of Czechoslovakia. It used to be a magnificent castle. There is the legend of Saint Georg slaying the dragon that has been recreated as a play, the annual Drachenstich, every year for over one hundred years. It is told that a huge dragon came over across the border of Bavaria from Czechoslovakia. The beautiful princess from the castle saved the people by allowing them to take shelter inside the castle. Then she sent a knight in shining armor to slay the dragon and save the surrounding town. The brave knight charged the dragon while riding a stately stallion and threw a long spear down its throat as it roared and spewed fire and smoke into the air. Of course the knight always won leaving the giant dragon bleeding and dead on the ground. The modern day dragon is made of paper mache and is twice as big as the jeep that it encloses. It blows smoke out of its huge nostrils and it spits fire out of its gigantic mouth. It's tail swings to and fro from sidewalk to sidewalk as it moves down the street. Today only the castle's tower remains standing and is a museum. As far as Margot is concerned, she is the royal princess who saved the magical town. She loved her world and everything in it. It was all she knew, but it was all she ever wanted (her family and her little village surrounded by mountains).

"Margot! Get out of the clouds. We are leaving for home. Don't fall behind and let that wild boar catch you. There are no trees with boards close by to climb," yelled Ilse. "Remember what day it is tomorrow. Our school will be greeting the Furher at the train station in the morning."

That brought Margot back to reality. This was the Furher's first visit to their little town. Margot and Ilse barely slept all night.

Early Monday morning in 1938 her class walked to the little train station in her little village of Furth im Wald, Germany. It was a gorgeous day and all the school children had to bring a bouquet of flowers to greet their impelling leader. Margot was dressed in her Sunday best with a ring of flowers around her head. She stood with her hands tightly locked around her bouquet. She almost squeezed the life out of the colorful flowers she had ready for him. She felt suspended in time as she waited for the train to come to a complete stop. Suddenly her legs were shaking uncontrollably. There he was, the one who would lead the German people to prosperity and give them hope, the Fuhrer, Adolf Hitler. He stepped off the train and glanced at the waiting children. As he came toward her, the first thing she noticed was his piercing blue eyes. He took her flowers and slowly kissed her cheek. It all seemed like slow motion. She could not believe he kissed her cheek out of all the other children. After gathering some more flowers, he turned toward the townspeople and spoke with a forceful and thundering voice. Something about making the greatest achievements in German history and that it was God's will and the people loved him. She didn't understand all of his words, but the people at the train station seemed to be hypnotized by them. His voice rang through her ears and she thought, *am I supposed to be hypnotized too? He sure is a small man to be so powerful.* Then everyone shouted "Sieg Heil!"

She did not wash her cheek for a week. She just stared at it in the mirror and wondered if there was something magic about it. All the people at the train station seemed to think there was something remarkable happening. She had no clue about the monster they were all worshiping.

DEATH OF LUDWIG

Today seemed like any other day as Ilse and Margot walked home from their first day back in school. It was 1939 and summer was almost over. A few black clouds were hanging low in the sky releasing cold drops of rain on their heads. They used their books for cover and quickly ran towards home. They were both out of breath as Ilse opened the door and called to their mother, "Mommy, we're home. Where are you?" No one answered and the living room door was closed. Margot put her ear against the door, "It sounds like someone is crying." Just then their oldest sister, Luise and her new husband, Gerhard, opened the door and motioned them to follow into the kitchen. Luise was 19 and so beautiful with her long wavy hair. Margot was especially crazy about her new brother-in-law. She thought he was as charming as a prince and that the two of them looked so perfect together. Luise turned to face the two girls and they noticed a tear trickling out of her eye. By the way she was clenching her mouth, they could tell she was holding back her tears.

"Where's Mommy? What's happened?" asked Margot. By now she was getting scared. She looked over at Ilse's colorless face and knew something was terribly wrong. "Why is the hay wagon out front?"

"That's how they brought Father home from the factory," answered Luise, "He's in the bedroom with the doctor."

"There's been an unfortunate accident," added Gerhard. "Your father has been hurt at work. One of the large suspended mirrors hanging from the ceiling fell on him and he has a concussion. The doctor thinks he may have a blood clot in his brain."

"Is that bad?" asked Margot already knowing the answer.

The doctor opened the bedroom door and called for Maria, "He wants to see his family now."

Maria, Luise, Ilse and Margot all entered the bedroom where poor Ludwig was lying. It was heart-breaking for them to see him in so much pain. As they stood around him, Margot saw something she will never forget. Her father's eye's never frightened her before, but this time as she looked into them, she saw a veil, a kind of film over his eyes. She stood in absolute horror as she realized she saw Death in his eyes. "My little blue bird," he said to Margot, "you are in the early morning sunrise of your life, the very beginning. Live your life like a sweet song, like the blue bird sings. Choose songs from your heart that will brighten your day like the morning sun's luminous glow as it ascends upward in the sky." She barely comprehended his peculiar words as he took her hand and gave it a squeeze. "Be good to your mother and sister," he continued as he handed her a little Bible, "always keep it with you because it is special. Whenever you need my advice and cannot ask me, look inside and read the pages. It will be your comfort."

Margot was too shocked to speak. She took the Bible and just tried to nod her head. "This must be a most frightful dream. Any minute I'll wake up and all will be well," she thought to herself.

For three exhausting days Maria never left Ludwig's side running out of the room only to get a cool wet cloth for his sweltering face. Margot felt entirely helpless. She could only pace the floor as her two sisters kept themselves busy cooking food or cleaning the house. Sometimes Ludwig knew who his wife was and sometimes he didn't. On the third day, the doctor called them all into the bedroom. They all stood by his bed holding hands. Ludwig had a faraway look in his glassy eyes as he lashed his arm into the air, "Not yet," he cried out. "I'm not ready. Go away."

"Who me?" asked Maria. "Are you talking to me, Ludwig?"

"No, not you," he said as his face smiled then suddenly changed as if it had fallen in and gotten smaller. It occurred to them that he had died as they watched. It was a frightening sight that they hoped never to experience again. "He was only 48 years old; too young to leave this earth," sobbed Maria.

As the doctor wheeled Ludwig out of the room, Maria panicked and ran after him. She held onto the cart trying to stop the doctor. "No, no don't take my Ludwig away! What will we do," she screamed as she pulled on the cart. "My God, why have you taken him away from us? Please bring him back. Let him live. I'll do anything, just don't take my beloved from me."

Margot was too numb to move. Her father was the world to her. He was her rock. "How can you leave me now when I am still so young?" she wailed. "I love you, Father! I need you! Please come back."

"We are going to miss him, Margot," said Luise. "Somehow we will all get through this if we help each other. I think you should come and stay with Gerhard and me for a while. You will like Cologne. It is a beautiful city with..." "No! I won't go," screamed Margot, "I want to stay here." She proceeded to stomp her feet. For the time being, she got her wish.

With her little Bible in her hand, Margot proceeded to run to the top of her little mountain and cried to God, "My God, where are you? Why did you take my father? I know he was in a lot of pain, but you could have helped him! Are you there? Are you real? Are you listening? How will we survive without him? What will we do?" Then she began to yell. Her scream would have woken the dead. Worn out, she sat on the ground and leaned against a tree. Half blinded by her warm tears, she suddenly saw a little blue feather falling, fluttering toward her. She wiped her swollen eyes and tried to focus. She followed the feather with her eyes and watched it gently land on top of her knee. Completely perplexed, she slowly opened her mouth and took a deep breath. She was not prepared for or expecting any kind of answer to her angry outbursts. Then she thought she heard a muffled whisper in her ear, "Be good my little bluebird." This caused her to jump to her feet and almost step on the delicate feather. She raised her head and with sorrowful eyes asked for forgiveness. She bent over and picked up the fragile blue feather and tenderly kiss it. She didn't know how long she stood there holding and caressing it, but it seemed like an eternity. The wind blew her disheveled hair and tickled her face. She smiled as she put the feather in her Bible and headed back home.

Only three weeks later, they heard the dreadful news on their radio. It was September 1, 1939 when Hitler attacked Poland with the use of an old battleship, the Schleswig-Holstein which pulled into the harbor by Danzig. Then came the air attacks, the Stukas which were dive-bombers and finally the army. By September 3, 1939, France and Britain declared war on Germany, but Poland had already surrendered. Maria, Ilse and Margot were stunned when they heard the word 'WAR'. Margot had just learned to smile again sitting in her new brother-in-law's lap. He even called her bluebird just like her father used to call her. Gerhard and Luise would come every weekend to visit them.

Maria had to clean people's houses to support Ilse and Margot. They were struggling to make ends meet and barely surviving. Whenever possible, Ilse and Margot tried to help by sweeping stairs and the sidewalks in front of the buildings. It still took all day to earn enough money to pay the rent and buy food. Almost every day after school Ilse and Margot would walk to the woods to gather wood for the stove. Before the weather got too cold they were able to fill their buckets with wild blueberries or strawberries. Maria cooked them or dried them. Sometimes when they had enough berries, they stood on the corner and sold them for a little bit of money. They also brought home the wild mushrooms for Maria to cook with. They were happy when they found sauerampfer (sorrel), a plant whose blue-green leaves cooked like spinach. Maria made a tasty soup out of them and added the leaves to other things she cooked like pancakes or sauce for potatoes. In the winter, the roots could be dug up and also used.

It was Margot's job to travel across town with her rucksack and gather the left over potatoes at Mr. and Mrs. Mueller's potato field. Lots of people came to dig or pick up the little potatoes left on the ground. Margot had known the Muellers all her life. Mrs. Mueller often saved a few plump potatoes for Margot to add to her rucksack which Maria would cut into thin slices to dry. They were like thick potato chips without the salt. Margot usually had some berries or mushrooms to give to Mrs. Mueller in exchange.

Going to the potato farm was one of the duties she thoroughly enjoyed. She could skip through the fields of blue, yellow and pink wild flowers and no one was there to bother her or tell her what to do. One day in late October, Margot was on her way home from Mrs. Mueller's with her sack of potatoes on her back. She decided to take a short cut through the edge of the woods to see if she could find some more wood to bring back. While she was gathering the kindling, she noticed the man hanging from the tree. He was swinging ever so slightly back and forth. Margot knew he must be dead and tried not to look up at him. Her pace grew swifter and she started to run. In haste she turned and looked back with a quick glance. The man's eyes were wide open and his tongue was hanging out of the side of his mouth. Margot dropped the kindling wood from her arms and kept running until she reached the door to her own room. She fell on her bed with the rucksack still on her back. The potatoes spilled out onto the floor.

"What is the matter with you?" asked Ilse.

"I just saw an awful sight," said Margot, "in the woods on the way home."

"Come and eat something girls," yelled Maria. "Margot where are you? Is that the door I heard slamming? What is going on?"

"I'm not hungry, mamma," shouted Margot.

Maria walked into the room. "Are you sick?"

"I don't feel so good right now. Maybe I'll eat something later. Ilse go eat with mother. I just want to stay here and lie down for a while," said Margot.

Every time she closed her eyes she could see the rope with the man and those eyes and the tongue hanging down. It scared her, but she didn't want to talk about it. She got out her little Bible and opened it to the page containing the little feather and started reading. It did usually make her feel better, but tonight she could not be consoled. She laid on her bed and waited to fall asleep.

Ilse came back with a bowl of soup and talked Margot into eating a few spoonfuls. She hugged Margot and laid down beside her on the bed. "We'll talk about it tomorrow little sister," she whispered. They both closed their eyes to get a night's sleep.

"Listen, Ilse," said Margot, "is that mommy crying again? She sure cries a lot."

"I know," said Ilse, "Mommy has too many worries to deal with since daddy died. We have to think of a way to help her more."

"What can we do, Ilse. You seem to understand the situation better than I do," replied Margot.

"In the morning we'll make mommy breakfast" said Ilse

"What can we make?" asked Margot.

"We'll figure everything out in the morning. That's what we'll do little sister," answered Ilse as she held Margot tightly.

GERHARD LEAVES FOR WAR

"No not yet! I haven't had you long enough. My heart is too young to fall into pieces. Let's run away to a faraway place where no one can find us so that I can hold you and never let you go" pleaded Luise suddenly unable to hold back a flood of tears.

Gerhard sat beside her and wept. It was truly the end of their beautiful romance. He had to go and he knew his heart and soul cried for more time with his lovely bride of nine months.

"Please tell me it is all a horrible joke," said Luise. "Why does our happiness have to fade away into the darkness of war and hate? Can't you wait until tomorrow? Maybe then it will turn out to be a loathsome dream that will go back to hell and stay there. It will all disappear and be forgotten."

"My sweet love, my treasure," whispered Gerhard. "If only we could close our eyes and make it all go away. My only dream is to be back in your arms and never leave you again."

Time stood still for just a moment as they embraced and gave each other a last kiss before the reality of life split them apart and turned their sweet song of love into sour notes of distress.

"No, don't go!" repeated Luise. "It's not fair. Why can't we just run away?"

"They would surely find me and kill us both. I have to go. Be brave for me. It will be very hard for both of us to part," said

Gerhard, "my heart hurts too and it will cry out in the night so loud that no matter where I am you will hear it, but we must stay strong for each other and remember that our love will keep us from going insane through all this madness."

"Come back to me my love. Please come back."

"I promise I won't get killed while fighting in this war," said Gerhard as he tightly held Luise for the last time. He kissed her tenderly trying to hide the deep pain he felt inside his very soul. All the fresh new dreams of their future together might never come to pass. He felt as if their precious dreams had been crushed like a cigarette butt thrown to the ground and trodden upon until all traces of it disappeared into the dirt. He wondered if there would even be a future. He couldn't handle such a thought and he couldn't let Luise know of his fear about it.

"What's wrong with this world? People are walking around with their eyes closed. Even when someone takes a peak, there's still a fog hovering over them," said Luise. "Why, Gerhard, why?"

"They are simply afraid to open their eyes, afraid of what they will see," answered Gerhard.

"All this killing makes me ashamed to be a human being," said Luise. Tears came rolling out of her eyes like a rushing waterfall. Gerhard bit his lip to hold back his feelings of hurt and fear. "You'll see," said Gerhard, "We'll be back together again soon. All will be okay and we'll continue with our dreams of a family and children."

Luise suddenly found herself embracing Gerhard with a tight grip. Their hearts pounded in unison as their lips met with a passionate kiss. She felt the angels crying as her river of tears melted into her heart. Their minds and bodies became like one as their souls united with their love. All else was silent; savoring their last great moment. Unable to move, Gerhard said, "I've just had a taste of heaven that I will never forget and my dream will be of this moment every time I close my eyes."

"As will mine," whispered Luise.

As Gerhard gathered himself together, Luise put a picture of herself and Gerhard in a small empty matchbox. A note was wrapped around the picture that said, "I will be waiting for you to come back to me. Your one and only true love, Luise." She handed it to Gerhard. "When you feel like you cannot go on, look at the picture and remember you are not alone. I am here," said Luise with hope in her frightened heart. Gerhard clasped the matchbox with the picture in his hand forcing his quivering lips to fabricate a smile as he left his beautiful, tender love to walk into a violent, monstrous world of war.

HISTORY UNFOLDS

Germany has been very vulnerable since the end of World War I. First, King Kaiser Wilhelm was forced to give up his throne and run for his life to Holland because he was accused of promoting the war. This caused the government to be blown to pieces. Now they have nothing. The people had grown accustomed to a monarchy and were at a loss as what to do next. In the 1920's, Germany went through one government after another. Sometimes within a few months there would be five different governments and none of them had worked. Some experts say that the treaty of Versailles (which ended WWI) was a direct cause of World War II. France and England were out to get Germany. They had lost millions of dollars and a whole generation of men. They were not going to let Germany get away with all the destruction. Although the Versailles Peace Treaty blamed Germany for WWI, Austria-Hungary actually started it bringing Germany in as their ally. However, since Germany kept fighting after Austria-Hungary backed out, they had to take full blame. The Treaty reduced the German army to bare minimum. They even had to sink most of their own navy ships. Cash money was paid to Britain and France for many years. They even had to give them most of their natural resources such as coal and timber. And now Germany's economy has been crushed. Their sense of national worth has been destroyed. They are told they are the scum of the earth, no better than worms. Money has become worthless, so the people are suffering and struggling. They are ripe and ready to listen to anyone who had an answer to their problems.

Lots of people spoke at the beer halls offering solutions, but only one man brought along his body guards to make certain he was heard above all the rest. He claimed to have a vision of a new and better Germany. He had all the answers and he forced the people to listen. He said he knew how to bring Germany back to its feet. He said, "We will have an army and we will have jobs. We will rule the earth. And the fault of all our suffering are the Jews." It is so unfortunate that when people are desperate, they look for a scapegoat. But the worst thing was that he was able to get away with it even though some of the people at the Versailles Peace Treaty were Jewish.

Maybe if Germany had been allowed a healing time or if France, England and Italy had not been so harsh after WWI and if they had helped Germany's economy and self-respect instead of destroying it, Germany would not be so desperate and destitute as to fall into the evil hands of Adolph Hitler. By the time the citizens of Germany realized what he was really up to, it was too late. He had the country under complete control and his "robots" did everything he told them to do. They are afraid to talk; he had ears everywhere. He probably killed as many of his own people as the war itself. People are killed simply for saying something he did no want to hear. Fear took over and Hitler knew how to use it.

In 1933, Hitler formed the Hitlerjugend (Hitler youth) to toughen up the youngsters of the country with sports and rough outdoor living like camping and hiking. The youth were filled with propaganda and patriotism is pounded into their heads. He forced all of Germany's teachers to join the National Socialist Teacher's league and swear to be loyal and obedient to Hitler. No Jewish teachers were allowed.

Hitler's invasion of Poland in September of 1939 drove Great Britain and France to declare war on Germany. They had guaranteed military support for Poland if attacked by Germany.

By 1940, the German army invaded Holland, Denmark, Norway, Belgium, Luxembourg, France and Romania. They continued their Blitzkrieg (lightning war) attacks on Britain's factories and airfields. Hitler said he needed "Lebensraum" living space for his idea of the pure German race. He would surprise and strike with lightning speed using dive-bombers (stukas), tanks and motorized artillery including interrupting the enemy's communications. This would shock and disorient the enemy in order to trap and immobilize them.

AFTER GERHARD
LEFT FOR WAR

The days and weeks blended into one and seemed to continue forever. Time seemed to turn into an enemy that Luise was powerless against. She proceeded to carry on as if she were alive, but inside she felt half dead with only hope for her tired soul to cling to. She diverted her attention to her elderly neighbors whom she checked in on almost every day. She was frightened for them because they were Jewish. They were the Bernsteins and she had grown very fond of them. She could call on Mr. Bernstein to fix almost anything and dinners weren't so lonely when they invited her to join them. They tried not to bring up war news in their discussions, but times were getting ever more fearful and they needed to pay attention to all that was happening around them. Their only resource was the news that the German government would broadcast.

In the summer of 1941, Hitler began his Holocaust. Jews are ordered to wear yellow stars. They and others such as gypsies are considered undesirables. Many tens of thousands are shipped to concentration camps in overcrowded trains. By 1941, Hitler ordered the extermination of the Jews calling it Endlosung (the final solution). The German public was mostly unaware of the horrors because Goebbels created a propaganda campaign showing bogus films portraying Jews living happily on farms at the concentration camps. Some Germans guessed the truth, but most did not want to think or believe the unthinkable.

Luise was getting more and more anxious for the Bernsteins

and tried to talk them into moving to a safer place, but they stood their ground. "This has always been our home. We won't leave," they said one morning as Luise told them about a plan to relocate them. "But I found someone who can hide you and take care of you," she said. "Please reconsider."

"We are too old now and not worth all the trouble. No one will come for us. We are practically on death's door anyway," they said.

"I won't have you talking with such pitiful words. You've got to go," said Luise.

The Bernsteins were stubborn, but Luise never gave up trying to save them until that dreadful day. They were stolen away in the middle of the night to be taken only God knows where. Luise's imagination could never go to such a depth of hatred as the Bernsteins were headed toward. Mankind was sinking into its own self destruction and she was completely powerless against it. She only knew she must carry on for Gerhard's sake.

Finally, her first letter came. "My dear treasure," it said. "I cannot and will not tell you of all the death that surrounds me. Only that I miss you dearly. You are my only connection to what I remember of love. Please wait for me. I should get a leave in a few months. I think for a week. I will look forward to holding you and loving you. As always, your love forever, Gerhard."

She read his letter every night before she fell asleep and pretended he was lying there beside her holding her in his arms. This is the way she kept love in her heart. "Only love can conquer wickedness and hate," she thought. "Only love will triumph and endure. Hatred will only destroy itself in the end.

AIRPLANE CHAPTER

Although Margot and her family were away from the big city, their little village of Furth im Wald felt the burdens of war. Food provisions were few as supplies were hard to deliver. The bomb scares were closer together and such fear had spread throughout Germany that even neighbors could not be trusted. Times were indescribable.

Margot and Ilse arrived home from school earlier than usual. Ilse turned to hug Margot as they walked inside, but Margot was visibly shaken and ran straight into her room. "Why are you crying my little one?" asked Maria.

"I don't want to talk about it." Margot stated, "I just want to forget it ever happened."

"Has someone hurt you? How can I help you if you don't tell me what's wrong?"

"It's just that I'm so confused that I don't know what to think anymore. Aren't we suppose to love everyone like it says in the Bible, Mamma? Father always said to forgive people and even if you don't understand try not to judge them."

"Yes, Margot, what happened that was so terrible," asked Maria.

"Well," continued Margot, "we were sitting at our desks at school doing our school work when all of a sudden we heard a loud thunderous crash. We all ran to the window instead of taking cover. The teacher told us to sit down, but when we saw the broken airplane coming to a halt in the schoolyard, we just had to run outside to get a closer look. The teacher said it was a British plane. The pilot was just hanging out of the smashed window. It frightened me, but at the same time as I looked at his bloody face with little bits of glass embedded in his skin, I actually felt sorry for him and started to cry. That made the teacher really angry. She told me that we were not allowed to cry for the enemy and made me spit on him. Then she punished me with her stick and said, "I'll give you a real reason to cry. As she grabbed my pigtails and pulled me, the SS soldiers showed up. I recognized one of them as the school teacher's boyfriend. I saw them sneak a quick kiss once."

"Did the teacher hurt you, Margot?" asked Maria.

"I don't know what she would have done if the soldier hadn't have shouted, "Hey what are you doing with that girl?" answered Margot. "The teacher said she is punishing me and that I need to learn that feelings for the enemy will not be tolerated. He walked up to me and asked me if I learned my lesson."

"What did you say?" asked Maria.

"Of course I turned toward the soldier straight and tall, wiped my tears and said Yes, I will not cry for the enemies of Germany. The soldier seemed to be satisfied and told the teacher to let me go. He said that I understand my mistake now. She reluctantly let me go and I ran inside. What am I suppose to feel about the pilot? I tried to hate him, but his sad, beaten up face kept popping into my mind and I didn't want to hate him. Does that make me a good or bad person?"

"My poor little girl. At ten years old you already have to decide such adult things," said Maria. "No one can change what you feel in your heart. You are not good or bad, just a loving, compassionate human being. Always listen to your heart when you face such a decision. It will never lead you wrong. As for the teacher, she only did what she considered the right and proper thing to do at the time. She sees the situation differently because she is an adult and we are at war. Under different circumstances and different times she might have reacted quite the opposite."

"You made me feel better, mamma, just like daddy used to do. Why did he have to die and leave us alone just when we needed him the most? What do you think they'll do with the pilot and the airplane?" asked Margot.

"There's a lot I know, but much more I don't know, Margot. By Monday morning when you go back to school, it'll all be gone. Let's have our dinner now, then you and Ilse can get ready for bed. You've had a hard day."

Maria served dinner and Margot was up to her usual antics. "Potatoes again," she complained, "I'm sick of potatoes, dried potatoes, potato pancakes, potato peel cake. I wouldn't be surprised if potatoes are growing in my stomach. I just want to throw up."

I'll eat yours," added Ilse, "we're having potato soup tonight."

"Okay, okay I'm hungry enough to eat it. Sorry mamma, I lost myself for a minute," said Margot.

"Well, come find yourself before I eat yours," yelled Ilse.

Potato soup wasn't so bad after all. Margot had a second bowl. Then it was time to get ready for bed. "Mamma, how are we supposed to brush our teeth? We don't have any toothpaste left. When will we get some more?"

"Children, I don't know. Let's see what we can find for you to clean your teeth with. Any ideas:" said Maria.

"How about soap?" said Ilse.

"That awful, stinky gunk. It doesn't even feel good when you clean yourself with it and it makes you smell like a dirty putrid shoe. We can go outside and use some dirt. It is gritty and it might clean off our teeth if we rinse out our mouth real good after we use it," said Margot with a wide grin on her face.

"That is an ingenious idea, but we still have a little bit of salt left. Put a drop of water and a tiny pinch of salt on your toothbrush and clean your teeth with it," declared Maria, "We'll figure out something better for tomorrow my Lieblings."

The two girls bound for the sink and did what their mother instructed. "Well, it's better than dirt I guess and it is fairly gritty," protested Ilse.

"It is almost bearable, but I hope we don't have to do this every night," grumbled Margot. "I'll race you to bed."

CANDY ON DESK

Life goes on. Many children still went to school and some people still went to work. Margot remembered sitting at her school desk one cold morning reflecting on her problems. It was Tuesday, October 15, 1941 and tomorrow was her birthday. She would be eleven years old and her father wouldn't be there. She really needed his caring arms that morning on her way to school. The air was crisp as she walked out the door and started her usual journey alone that day as her sister, Ilse, was sick. As she arrived toward the other end of town, she saw people wandering in circles and others frantically digging through the rubble calling to their loved ones. Her little town of Furth im Wald was hit by several screeching bombs the night before. She and her mother along with her sister were in the damp basement that night praying as hard as they could to a God that they often wondered even existed. He must have heard them last night though. They were safe for the time being. As she walked, she tried to keep her eyes directly in front of her, but she noticed something moving in the corner of her left eye. She turned and saw a waving arm sticking out of the ground. She bravely ran over to pull it out of the dirt but to her horror there was no body attached to it. Too disoriented to move, she closed her tearing eyes and stood in complete shock as she dropped the dead arm she was holding. She then acted on her first impulse and began running to the other side of the world. She was too dazed to see the dead body in front of her. She turned to look as she tripped over it and will never forget the fear she felt as she tumbled to the ground. She felt so alone that moment. She wanted to call out to her father whom she missed so much, "help me, please," but she knew he wouldn't answer her. She didn't remember how she found her way back to school, but she found herself sitting in her seat. All she knew is that she wanted this day to be over.

Suddenly, the teacher startled everyone by demanding their attention. As the students looked up at her stern hard face, she said, "Now close your eyes and pray to God for a piece of candy." When the students were told to open their eyes and look at their desks, there was no candy. Next, she said," Close your eyes and pray to Hitler for a piece of candy." This time when they opened their eyes there was a piece of candy on their desks. There were only girls in her school and she wondered if the boys were getting the same treatment. Some of the bewildered girls looked around as if searching for something mysterious, but most of them knew that there was nothing puzzling about it. "We are too old to be fooled by such a stunt," thought Margot almost insulted. "We are not little innocent children anymore. We've learned too much about life and death."

"Go ahead" said the teacher, "It is safe to eat your candy." As the children opened their wrappers, the teacher continued, "We have an important assignment today. We must gather together and walk to the woods in an orderly fashion. Our job is to pick up all the poison candy thrown down from airplanes by one of our enemies, the British. Everyone collect your jacket and follow me." It almost looked like a long parade as the girls marched in procession down the street. Margot was used to the long walks to the woods. She went there as often as she could because it reminded her of the times she and her father would search for mushrooms. When they arrived at their destination, Margot noticed that the boys were already there. The teacher handed everyone a clothes pin and a bag. The children quickly went to work. They worked until dusk until they heard the blowing of a whistle that meant they could stop. The teachers gathered up all the children and marched them back to the school. They were all given a drink of watered down milk and sent home.

Margot ran all the way back to the apartment to tell Ilse and her mother everything that had happened. "The one thing that I don't understand, mamma, is what the teacher told us about the Jews. She talked about a competition between Jews and Aryans. Isn't competition good? She made it sound liked the Jews were bad." After much contemplation, Margot recalled what her father had once told her, "It doesn't matter what other people say you are. What matters is what you believe yourself to be."

HANS AND GERDA

Hans and Gerda had already lived through what was called the biggest war anyone had ever known, WWI. From 1914 to 1918, Hans fought bravely in the muddy trenches. The more he tries to forget, the more his memories keep coming back to haunt him. His memory brings him back to one dark night when there was no moon. Hans and some of his infantry crawled across the ground to raid the enemy. They threw bombs into their trench and stayed ready to club them if they came out. This maneuver was very dangerous and most of his infantry did not make it back. The other side would do the same which made it hard to sleep at night. They had to be on continual watch. During their breaks from trench duty, the men finally got to sleep.

Once after a number of cold rainy days staying soaked in the muddy water that had gathered in his trench, Hans was taken to a nearby hospital to treat his red swollen feet. Hans let his feet stay wet and cold too long. He had heard about other men losing feeling in the foot or even losing toes. He was brought back for foot washings and bed rest. He was more careful to keep his feet dry after that ordeal.

Hans and Gerda were both teachers. Gerda preferred working with the little kindergartners, but Hans enjoyed teaching the older children. His love for mathematics inspired his students.

Hans and Gerda found each other while hiking on a footpath along the Ahr River. During his usual hike, Hans noticed the beautiful young Gerda a short distance in front of him. It started to rain and the sudden thunder and lightning frightened Gerda. Her pace quickened into a run. Hans ran after her and quickly caught up. He grabbed her hand and ran with her down the path to shelter. They since celebrated many of their anniversaries at the place they met.

GERHARD HOME ON LEAVE

Margot was so excited to once again take a trip to Cologne and visit her sister, Luise. Her brother-in-law, Gerhard, was coming home on leave for a whole week. It had been a year since his last leave in 1941. He would see his little son for the first time. Little Gerhard Gunther Thomas was already three months old. Maria and Ilse would accompany Margot just overnight and Gerhard would bring Margot back at the end of his leave. They packed their small bags and walked to the train station.

"I can't wait to take the baby for a walk and give him his bottle," said Margot.

"I wish I could stay longer," said Ilse.

"You had your time with Luise when the baby was born," said Maria. "You stayed two weeks to help your sister."

"Ya, now it's my turn," announced Margot.

They hurried to purchase their tickets as the train was already at the station. Margot usually slept like a baby in a carriage so it didn't seem like a long trip when the train finally pulled to a halt five hours later. Gerhard was waiting with his little cart ready to transport their baggage to his cozy little apartment. "I hope you haven't been waiting too long. It seemed to take forever this time," said Maria anxiously stepping down off the train. " I don't know how Margot can sleep with all the noise."

"I enjoyed the wait. It was nice to have some time to relax and just rest a bit," said Gerhard. "You three must be hungry and some of you tired by now. Luise bartered for a chicken from the neighbor across the street."

"Oh my, she shouldn't have done that. What did she give the neighbor for it?" asked Maria.

"Just an old necklace that she never wore. Nothing to worry about," said Gerhard, "hurry along now children your sister is waiting to see all of you."

Luise was adding more kindling to her wood-burning stove when the four entered the kitchen. The table was set with her best silverware and tablecloth. She was rewarming the food, which she so carefully prepared.

"Oh what a nice meal you have ready for us! Such thoughtfulness is rare these days, especially when you really cannot afford it," said Maria.

"It was worth it just to see a smile on your face, mamma," said Luise, "let's enjoy it while we can. I missed you and my little sisters too. I'm so glad you're here."

After dinner, Ilse and Margot sat on the couch and took turns holding baby Gunther. He was just learning to coo and laugh.

The night flew by and morning came too quickly, but Maria and Ilse were on their way back home to little Furth im Wald with a piece of bread and a chicken leg to nibble on during their trip. Gerhard made sure they were safely on the train before he headed back home.

"Are you up for a long walk, my little bluebird?" asked Gerhard as he walked in the door to the apartment. "I need to visit my cousin's farm to get some milk for the baby. Maybe he'll let you milk a cow."

"I'm always ready to follow you wherever you go. I have missed you so much. Is Luise and the baby coming with us?"

"Not this time. They'll wait for us at home."

"I hope they give us a few eggs also. I have the bracelet that matched the necklace if you need it," said Luise.

"Don't be ridiculous," replied Gerhard, "My cousin wouldn't ask me for anything. Put your bracelet away."

As they crossed the Cologne bridge, Margot stopped to look over the side at the water, "Can we take the baby for a walk later down by the river?" she asked.

"Maybe tomorrow. We have a long day ahead and we'll get back too late," answered Gerhard.

It was a long walk to the farm, but Margot didn't mind the fast pace. She was looking forward to seeing the cows and horses. "My tummy is growling like a lion," said Margot, "I can't wait to have a real glass of milk instead of that blue looking awful stuff mamma has at home."

"I know it is hard to drink the watery milk they give you, but there is not enough for everyone now, so they need to thin it down to make it go further," replied Gerhard. "Look, see the narrow stream up ahead? When we were younger, my cousin, Franz and I used to drink out of it. Then we would climb that tree and watch the cows."

"Did you ride the horses? Maybe Franz will let me ride too. How many are there?" asked Margot.

"There are five and a little colt. Be careful around him, new colts can be very feisty. I remember one that kicked me so hard I tumbled down the hill and landed in the stream. Don't laugh. It really hurt," exclaimed Gerhard.

"I'm sorry my dear brother-in-law, I won't laugh anymore," said Margot as she jumped across the small stream and ran up the hill toward the rustic farmhouse. She was overjoyed when she saw the frisky colt running toward her. She stopped to pick some green grass to feed him. She held out her hand toward the colt, but he backed away. Margot stepped toward him too quickly and startled him. He suddenly bit her outstretched hand and made her finger bleed. Gerhard saw the whole incident, but was still too far away to prevent it. He didn't know his feet could run so fast. He was so used to the straight leg marching.

"My finger is not hurt real bad. I shouldn't have scared him. I forgive him. He didn't know any better. He's just a baby horse," whispered Margot.

"We've got to get into the house to clean your hand," said Gerhard as he lifted Margot into his arms. Already out of breath, he raced to the farmhouse where he was greeted by Franz and his wife, Helga. They cleaned and bandaged her little bleeding finger. "Do you think she'll live?" asked Gerhard.

"Oh, I think she will survive especially when she sees what's on the table for her," answered Franz. "We have fresh ripe tomatoes, green beans and strawberries from the garden."

Margot first asked if she could bring some back to Luise before she stuffed herself. The rest of the day was a great learning experience. Margot collected eggs, fed chickens, pitched hay, weeded the garden and learned to milk cows. She and Gerhard left with a dozen eggs and a basket full of fresh vegetables. The two tired bodies started their trek back home. Their quick pace slowly turned to a snail's pace as they crossed the bridge again near home. The apartment was a heavenly sight as they walked warily through the open door. Luise hurriedly cooked eggs and vegetables for dinner. Then Margot plopped into the feather down bed with eyes half closed. She only managed to read one page of the little Bible her father had given her before her eyes closed shut sending her into a dream state. Then only a few hours later she was awakened by a blasting noise.

The sirens were a deafening sound to the ears especially in the hours before daylight. Even though Margot was used to hearing them, they still made her jump out of her skin. She was sound asleep and reluctant to get out of her warm bed. But she knew she must move quickly and could do it without thinking. She grabbed her robe, which she kept folded at the bottom of her bed. "I loathe that sound! It makes my ears ring and scrambles my brain."

"Turn out the lights Margot," yelled Luise in a slight panic. Gerhard ran to pull the curtains shut. "Light the candle by the basement stairs and grab your suitcases," demanded Gerhard. Luise snatched the baby and they all ran downstairs with their already packed suitcases containing extra clothes, identification papers and ration cards. Everyone in the apartment house had their own little space. Some had cots and others had old chairs or blankets to sit on. Luise and Gerhard had a little round table and two kitchen chairs in their corner. Their little closed-up box had blankets and pillows and other needed necessities. There was no heat in the basement and sometimes they had to spend hours down there.

"I forgot my little Bible from Father," cried Margot. "Can we run up to get it."

"No!" shouted Luise, "Are you crazy? Why isn't it in your suitcase?"

"I left it on the nightstand by the bed," answered Margot.

Gerhard whispered in Margot's ear and took her by the hand. "We'll be right back," he said to Luise. They ran upstairs as fast as they could. Margot headed for the bedroom and Gerhard's curiosity motivated him to peek out the window to see what was going on. "Come quickly, Margot. Look at this!" He opened the curtain and they watched as the sky was lit up like daytime. "What in the world is that Gerhard," asked Margot. "It looks like sparkling lights on Christmas trees floating down from the sky right below the moon."

"It surely does, bluebird. They are the flares that the planes throw out to illuminate the ground. That way they can see where to drop the bombs," They only had a minute to spare, but for that moment, they forgot their fears and hardships and were reminded of a happier time.

Suddenly they were jarred back to the dreadful reality of the situation. They felt the entire foundation of the building shake under their feet. "Watch out!" screamed Gerhard as the window shattered and glass propelled through the room. Gerhard instinctively grabbed Margot as he flew down the stairs.

"That was a close one," said Margot wiping her brow. "Oh no! You're bleeding!"

"Go get the first aid packet I made up," said Luise as she put little baby Gunther down in his homemade cradle, "Gerhard has a piece of glass in his forehead." She cleaned and patched him up while Margot sat on an old bicycle nearby. Another loud boom and Margot was thrown like a projectile across the room. A little dazed Margot stood up and slowly wiped herself off.

Gerhard saw the expression on her face and started laughing. "It's not funny," scolded Margot.

"You weren't hurt and you have to admit, it's a bit amusing when you see someone unexpectedly flying through the air." chuckled Gerhard. "Come here and sit on my lap."

"My knee has a cut on it," scowled Margot as she climbed up.

"Let me see. I'll kiss that little knee and make it feel better," smiled Gerhard. Luise started singing Margot's favorite song, Kommt ein Vogel Geflogen (a little bird came flying). It was a children's song she sometimes sings at school.

The noise of war continued for two more hours and just as suddenly as it came, it was over. "We had better go outside and see what kind of damage was done," said Luise. "It's almost daylight." Hesitantly they climbed the stairs and stepped outside. Toward the east the sun was rising, but the glowing light was coming from somewhere else. All the way down the street the fires were burning making it feel like a hot oven. All was in sad shambles as the alarming damage of the bombings came to view. There were dead bodies buried under rubble with only a leg or an arm sticking out of the dirt. Some people were trying to dig out their loved ones and running in circles frantically calling out names. Margot was speechless as she looked around. She noticed someone with long brown hair almost completely buried except for the head. She ran as fast as she could when she saw its eyes wide open staring at her. "I'm coming," she yelled as her feet nearly left the ground almost flying in the air. "Here I..." but her heart stood still and sweat rolled from her forehead as her eyes looked down at the tainted ground. Her horrifying scream overshadowed all the rest as she realized the head had no body attached to it. Gerhard came running toward her. He scooped Margot up in his arms and she hid her frightened face in his chest. She began sobbing as he carried her back into the apartment house.

"I need to go back outside to help. Are you going to be okay?" asked Gerhard. The images were still fresh in Margot's mind. She could not talk. "Stay here inside. I'll be back as soon as I can."

Reluctantly, Gerhard left Margot and walked back outside into a burning hell. His heart sank as he watched the painful faces of the children digging through the shattered pieces of stone and bricks. They looked so lost and broken. The hopelessness of the situation was unbearable. He wished he could just create a miracle and end all the destruction of not only the buildings, but of people's lives.

He joined Luise who was motionless with the baby held tightly to her chest. "Why don't you and the baby go back inside and lie down my sweet wife," whispered Gerhard as his arm embraced her. She turned toward the door without speaking a word as Gerhard silently prayed for the strength to carry on. He was thankful his apartment house was still standing as he helped his neighbors dig through the ruins for loved ones and other valuables. Some fires were still burning and others smoldering causing a smoky atmosphere that made it hard to breathe. He didn't know where to turn next as he slowly made his way down the street. Everyone was busy clearing the road and a path to the houses left standing. Most of the people worked quietly as if in shock. Gerhard stopped to help a little boy about six years old covered in dirt from head to toe. He was trying to remove the debris that was trapping his mother and sister still in the demolished basement. What a good feeling he had when they finally reached them and were able to pull them out. Although scratched and bruised, they were okay. Gerhard slowly moved on further down the war torn street. He noticed a young mother standing stiff as a statue with two small children clinging tightly to her soiled dress. He walked over to them and asked if they were all right. The mother slowly lifted her head and tried to force a smile.

"Oh my God," said Gerhard with panic in his voice, "your face and arm are bleeding. How long have you been standing here? Where do you live? Is a family member nearby? What is your name?"

"Ah, my name is Anna and this is Karl and Elizabeth. My mother is still in the house. She didn't come outside with us? Will you see if you can find her?" asked Anna.

"Stay here. I'll go look," said Gerhard as he sadly turned and walked over the pile of rubble that used to be a house. He must have dug for an hour in the dirt and debris before he finally found what looked liked a small woman wearing a pink robe. The weight of the earth and stones had crushed and broken her skull. Gerhard cringed at the thought of touching such a sorrowful sight. He carefully placed his shirt over her head and pulled her out of the dirt. He tried to erase the picture of her broken body out of his mind before Anna could see the grief in his face. He laid the body down next to Anna and hesitantly lifted his shirt away from the face. Poor Anna was devastated as she recognized her mother. The blood left her shocked face and she turned a grayish pale.

"Children, stay where you are," yelled Gerhard. "I'll take care of your mother." He held on to Anna as her knees shook and buckled from beneath her. Her mouth opened automatically as she vomited the last bits of food still left inside her churning stomach. Still holding on to Anna, Gerhard lowered her onto the ground, then took off his undershirt to roll it up and use as a pillow for her head. He then pulled the body aside and began the tedious job of digging a shallow grave for Anna's mother. He had no shovel, so he used flat stones and his hands. It took him until dark to dig a hole deep enough to set her into the ground.

"I'm so sorry we have to bury her in such a dreadful manner and without a priest," said Gerhard in a sympathetic voice. He helped the children gather a pile of stones and two sticks to make a cross for the grave. "Mother," called the children, "we need to say a blessing for Oma. Please get up now."

Barely able to move, Anna gradually lifted herself up and joined the others. They all held hands and said the Lord's Prayer together.

"Do you have a place to stay tonight?" asked Gerhard.

"I could try to get to my sister's house in Hochkirchen about 6 km from here. Do you know if the train station got hit? Is it still running?"

"The train station is still there, luckily. The targets seemed to be all the chemical and machine factories. Tonight you should stay with my wife and me. Then tomorrow we'll see about getting you to your sister's place," suggested Gerhard. "My little niece is staying with us this week. I'm sure she'll have some fresh clothes for Elizabeth and my lovely wife is about your size. We'll do just fine. How about it Anna?"

"How can I refuse such a generous offer kind sir?" replied Anna. "Come along children. This kind- hearted man is giving us a place to sleep tonight."

"By the way, my name is Gerhard Thomas. I live about a mile south of here. Come Elizabeth jump on my back and I'll give you a ride. I'm sure you are exhausted. Karl, you let me know if you need to change places with your sister, Okay?"

"Yes sir," stated Karl with a hint of a smile.

By the time they reached the apartment house, little six year old Elizabeth was sound asleep. Eight year old Karl was still marching along "Luise, Margot," called Gerhard, "I am here with company. They need a place to stay tonight. This is Anna, Elizabeth and Karl."

"Oh my God!" exclaimed Luise. "Please come in. What happened to your face?"

"It's all such a blurr," said Anna. "The bombs came and we had to run. We didn't want to be trapped. I grabbed the children and my mother was right behind me I thought."

" Let me show you where you can clean up. I have bread and tomatoes left over from yesterday. Margot, would you mind giving up your room and sleep with me and Gerhard?"

"Oh sure. I don't mind," answered Margot. " How long will they stay?"

"Probably just tonight. Tomorrow I'll take them to the train station to go to Hochkirchen. Anna has a sister there."

"Gerhard, can I come with you tomorrow?" asked Margot, "and maybe take the baby in the stroller?"

"I don't know. As long as everything looks clear and good in the morning maybe you can come. The train station is only a few miles away and I think they are through bombing here for now," said Gerhard watching Margot jump for joy. "You look like a little yo-yo, up and down, up and down."

After they had eaten, Luise gave Anna and the children fresh clothes and showed them to the little spare room that will soon be baby Gunther's, They were so worn out after their long ordeal they could barely say thank you before falling asleep. Luise washed their dirty clothes and hung them up to dry over the kitchen sink while Gerhard looked for something to patch up the broken window. Margot washed dishes and cleaned up the kitchen.

"Come here my little sister," said Luise, "and give me a big hug. Everything will be all right. Gerhard will get the cot ready for you in our room. You can sleep by baby Gunther's crib tonight. Get your suitcase and please remember your little Bible from father. Gerhard and I will be coming to bed soon." Margot gladly did as she was told. She just wanted to go to sleep.

"Window all patched up. How are the children?" asked Gerhard.

"Everyone is in bed and fast asleep," answered Luise.

"Great!" exclaimed Gerhard as he sat on the couch and motioned Luise to join him. He put his arm around her tightly. Luise finally released her tears and sobbed on his shoulder.

"It'll be okay my precious treasure. I promise you that in time this will all go away and there will be a future again. We will dream again and love again like we use to do," said Gerhard. "Remember when we first met and we decided to take a long stroll in the woods on the little mountain near your home in Furth im Wald? We saw a little fawn hiding in the brushes. You were so excited and tried to take a picture. Just then the mother ran toward us and chased us away. We ran so fast that you tripped over a stump and skinned your knee."

"Yes and then you carried me to the stream and used your handkerchief to clean my bleeding knee," interrupted Luise. "If that wasn't enough, on our way back we were chased by a wild boar. I was so scared. I thought we would die that day. All I could think about was the boar ripping us apart. But my great protector saved me."

"Oh ya! We ran up the tree with the boards nailed to it just for such an occasion. We were lucky that day. We waited until that big mean swine left us alone. It seemed like a long time, but we finally climbed down and continued our walk, although a bit more cautious. Now you'll see. Luck was with us then and it is with us now. All this disaster will go away and the sun will shine again."

"You always know what to say to calm my nerves," whispered Luise.

"Let's get to bed and try to get some sleep," said Gerhard.

"Good idea. We're all frazzled and worn down. I love you," said Luise.

A DAY LATER

The next morning looked a little brighter. The sun was shining, the dark clouds vanished and the foul air was not as smokey. Luise gave Anna and the children all the food she could spare and the clothes she had washed. She laid baby Gunther in his stroller for Margot to push. A gentle breeze slowly cleared the air and the baby had not been taken for a walk in days. The children looked rested and they were in good spirits. Margot had a smile on her face and the walk with the other children would help keep her mind off the disturbing situation. Luise stayed home to look in on some of her neighbors. Five people walking together was enough she thought and they wouldn't be gone long anyway, just a few hours or so.

Margot pushed the stroller along trying to enjoy the walk. Gerhard was already sorry he took Margot with him. People were still cleaning rubble off the littered streets and a few crumbling buildings were still smoldering. She tried to look straight ahead and started singing to the baby. She knew she must carry on as usual and go on living life as normally as possible. She must act as if everything is going to be okay or she would go crazy. In school she had heard about a man and woman who had jumped off their balcony to their death. She didn't want to die before her time like her father did. She knew her father must be watching over her and she wanted to make him proud.

"Can I take a turn pushing the baby?" asked Elizabeth, "I never pushed a baby carriage before."

"Okay," said Margot reluctantly, "come over here beside me

and help me push. When you get used to it, I'll let you try it by yourself. Do you want to push also, Karl?"

"Oh, I'll let you girls handle it. I'm busy with Gerhard. He has a lot of interesting stories to tell me," said Karl.

Their walk seemed short as they arrived at the station. They all felt a kinship as they hugged and cried together. Margot pulled a little doll and a homemade top out from the blanket of the stroller to give to Elizabeth and Karl. They clutched their new toys with tears of joy. Besides their grandmother, they had lost all of what they owned when their apartment house was destroyed.

Gerhard bought Anna and her children tickets to Hochkirchen and helped them board the train. Anna was still in a daze, but she managed to find a seat with Karl and Elizabeth and wave goodbye. Gerhard felt guilty letting her leave in such a state, but she refused to stay any longer. She just wanted to be with someone in her family.. On the way to the station she told Margot and Gerhard how her husband was away fighting and that she had not heard from him for over nine months. Her mother, whom she had lived with since the war started, was her only comfort. All she had left was her sister. Besides, Gerhard wanted to be sure that Anna and the children would get to her sister's house while the trains were still running to Hochkirchen.

Margot and Gerhard watched the train leave and turned to head back. Margot was holding the baby to feed him his bottle as Gerhard pushed the empty carriage. She felt quite grown up as she walked with little Gunther in her arms. She reluctantly placed him back into his stroller when he fell asleep. The long walk tired him out. Margot pushed the stroller along walking over the Cologne bridge singing happily to the baby. Suddenly, the deafening sound of the sirens blasted in their ears. They heard the familiar, but frightening sound of airplanes coming down faster and faster. Gerhard quickly grabbed the baby and pulled Margot along as he ran off the bridge and fell to the ground. He lay on top of them as the high pitched hissing noise of a bomb came falling to the ground exploding the bridge. Pieces of broken wood and flying metal were soaring through the air like angry project-iles looking for a victim to impale. Just when matters seemed at their worst, the incessant bullets came shooting to the ground. Margot tried to cover her ears when she heard the screams and howls of innocent people as they lay on the ground in anguish, but nothing stopped the roar of the chaotic sounds all around her. She wished she could button up her ears and become totally deaf.

"Are you okay?" asked Gerhard as he carefully lifted himself up still holding the baby in his arms. The sudden shock as he turned and offered his hand to help Margot caused him to freeze solid.

"My leg hurts really bad," answered Margot still laying head down.

"Don't move," yelled out Gerhard as panic started to set it. "Your leg is covered with splinters from the bridge." His mind was unable to comprehend the unimaginable situation as he stood there motionless.

"Gerhard," shouted someone from the distance. "Is that you I see?" His old school teacher, Hans, came running toward them at lightning speed when Gerhard didn't answer. "Hellfire! We've got to get this girl to the hospital. I hope the blasted bombs missed it. Gerhard, take the baby home and meet me at the hospital. I'll take care of your little Margot until you get back."

"No!" shouted Gerhard as the reality of it all woke him up from his stupor. "I can't leave my little bluebird now."

"Well, give me the baby then and I'll take him home to Luise and meet you later. Get a hold of yourself and do what is neces-sary to get her to the hospital. I love you, my old friend so please take care."

Gerhard handed little Gunther over to Hans and turned to

pick up Margot. His heart broke when he saw blood dripping from her fragile, injured leg. Margot's bleached out face was foremost in his mind. He knew he must hurry, but he had to stop and assess the situation. He didn't want to touch her left leg with all the wooden splinters protruding from it. As he looked closer, he noticed one of the bigger ones had been driven right through to the other side. How could he pick Margot up without hurting her even more? He could see the pain in her face and tears running down her cheek as she tried to be brave. "I'm going to lift you up and carry you to the hospital. I'll try to be careful, so let me know if I hurt you."

"Ouch, I don't know if I could hurt more than I am already. This is the worst day of my life except when father died. It hurts. It burns like a fire. What's going to happen to me? I'm so scared," cried Margot before she finally passed out. Gerhard held her tight as he ran with his little sister-in-law down the war torn street. "I never should have let her come," he thought to himself. "I honestly thought they were done bombing and would not come back so soon. How could I have been so stupid! I should have known better." His tears came out like rain. He could barely see what was in front of him. Everything was just a blur. Luckily, he knew his way to the hospital or he would never get there. He tripped over debris and almost fell over a dead dog left in the street. He managed to recover his balance and continue running until he arrived at the hospital. He was more than grateful when his eyes saw the building was only slightly damaged. Margot was lying limp in his shaking arms as he walked through the open front door. The words, "help me," struggled out of his mouth and he tried to swallow to keep from choking. In his torturous confusion, he had never been so frightened in his life. He was absolutely petrified. He had been on the front lines fighting, killing and even being shot at, but this was very different. Someone he loved more than life itself was close to death and he found himself at a loss as how to cope with it all. "Please help," he continued until a nurse like a God sent came to his rescue. "All the rooms are full, but I have an empty bed in the next hallway," she said trying to calm Gerhard with a reassuring voice. He took a deep breath with a feeling of some relief and followed the nurse.

They had just removed an old woman from the bed whose heart had failed. Gerhard tried not to take her death on the bed as a bad omen. He carefully placed Margot on the clean sheets and stepped back to let the nurse look at her. "I don't know if we can save this leg. Even if we remove all the splinters, we might not have enough antibiotics to stop the infection. This will be a major operation," commented the nurse as she left to find a doctor.

Gerhard paced the floor and called out to God with a mighty voice of rage and fear, "How can you let this happen! She is only a little innocent girl! Why not me? I have lied and killed and done horrible things. I'm the one who deserves this kind of torture. Why her? You are not a loving God. You are a heartless God."

"Stop it! Don't say it. Tell God you are sorry right now," exclaimed Margot as she opened her eyes. "God didn't do this. He loves us. Father would be angry to hear such raving and disrespect."

"My little bluebird! You are awake! I'm sorry. I lost my head. I was so afraid of losing you. Please don't be angry with me," apologized Gerhard.

"Don't worry. Father will watch out for me. He will ask God to make me well," said Margot.

"Here comes the doctor," said Gerhard, "lie still."

"Hi little one. I see you are in a big mess," said the doctor. "Half the bridge decided to visit your leg."

"It hurts. I want my mamma," cried Margot.

The doctor took Gerhard aside, "she's lost a lot of blood and I don't know if I can save her leg. It would be better to just cut it off right now and save her the pain and complications she'll have later."

"NO, NO! I won't let you," said Gerhard in a low voice so Margot wouldn't hear. "How can a little girl grow up without a leg. She couldn't run or ride a bicycle or dance with only one leg. Now I beg you. In God's name you have to save her leg!"

"'She may never walk normally. She may limp and it might hurt on top of that," said the doctor. "Could you live with that?"

"I'll take the chance!" yelled Gerhard.

Just then Hans and Luise came in to find Gerhard and Margot.

"Here we are," said Gerhard. "Maria must be told what has happened to her little girl. I'll have to go fetch her right away, but how can I leave little bluebird like this?"

"I'll go," said Hans, "I'll get Margot's mother and sister. I'll find a way to get there."

"Are you sure you are up for such a trip?" asked Gerhard. "You are almost 80 years old now?"

Without hesitation Hans replied, "Don't insult me. I'm as healthy as a horse."

"Ja, a dead one," mumbled Gerhard with a little chuckle.

"What was that?" asked Hans. "I'll leave first thing in the morning just before daylight. The bombs blew up the train soon after it left the station. I don't know how many people were killed, but the wreckage looked bad."

"Oh no!" exclaimed Gerhard. "Anna, Elizabeth and Karl! Don't tell Margot about the train yet. The war was suppose to be over by now. I've had such little time with my precious baby boy. I trust you'll get to Furth im Wald safely and bring Maria and Ilse back."

After the doctor did a thorough exam on Margot, he came over to Gerhard and Luise. "My heart hurts for you, but, I ask again to give me permission to end her misery. I need to cut her left leg off. It'll save a lot of suffering later down the road. Eventually we'll have to cut it off anyway. It'll become infected and the infection could spread and kill her. I might be able to save it down to the knee. The splinter that penetrated her leg is under the knee."

"What are you saying?" asked Gerhard, "Margot is not going to live life with a missing leg if I have to cut my own off to save hers!"

"Now, now calm down. I'll do my best," said the doctor. "I'm just trying to save her from a life of pain. I'll be back in a few hours. I have other emergencies to tend to first."

"Wait! To save a little girl's life, isn't that a crucial emergency? You've got to do it now! It can't wait!" demanded Gerhard.

"First of all, you can't tell me what to do," said the doctor a little angry. "Second of all, I said I have other people ahead of you. Now get out of my way!"

"In God's name please take her first. I beg you on my knees," pleaded Gerhard as he lowered his body to the floor. "I'll be going back to fight for Germany, our homeland. I do this not only for Margot, but for you too. I could die at anytime. Please, you have the power to let her live now. What else can I do?"

"All right, all right, she goes first. I only hope I have enough anesthesia and antibiotics left for that little girl to get through it all. You better be praying if you believe in anything," sighed the doctor.

Luise suddenly interrupted, "I feel a strong need to pray. I'm going to the chapel up on the hill. Do you want to come with me and the baby? It will take quite a long time for the doctor to operate on Margot."

"I just can't. I honestly don't know how I feel right now about

God or anything," answered Gerhard.

"I can stay here with you. I don't have to go to the chapel," said Luise.

"Yes you do, my treasure. Pray for both of us," requested Gerhard and he gave her a loving kiss.

Gerhard nervously paced the floor unaware of all the chaos and frenzy around him. He found himself thinking about the past when all was calm and peaceful. He reflected upon the time when he and Luise first met. He was pushing her on a swing in late August. The setting sun left brilliant colors in the glowing sky and love filled his heart.

"Higher, higher," shouted Luise, "I want to touch the sky."

"No, no," replied Gerhard. "I don't want you that far away from me. Come here you lovely creature." He grabbed the swing and swooped her up in his arms.

"Don't call me a creature," laughed Luise.

"What do you want me to call you?" asked Gerhard.

"Well, I'm no animal, but I'm not sure about you," she said as he started to swing her over his shoulder. "Put me down," she yelled as he twirled her around in a circle.

"Okay, but only if you promise to kiss me," he said.

"Oh yes, yes, you are the creature, not me," she said as he held her tightly and looked deeply in her eyes. "I'll be the creature and you will be my treasure," he said. "See that star? There it is. Our lucky star for a long happy life together." As their eyes met they were both spellbound and could not move for they wanted this moment to last forever. He pulled her closer until their bodies touched. He felt a fire for her ignite within him and he slowly kissed her neck. He remembered the smell of her freshly washed hair as he took a deep breath to drink in the moment.

Suddenly, Gerhard was brought back to the present moment by a tap on the shoulder rousing him from his blissful dream state. He found himself sitting on the floor by Margot's empty bed. Luise had her hand out ready to help him up. The baby was sleeping in her other arm. Back on his feet, Gerhard, took the baby from Luise and held him. "Did you pray at the chapel?" he asked.

"I prayed and prayed to God that Margot's leg will heal and be normal again. Do you believe God hears our prayers and grants them to the people that need help? I believe God told my heart that my little sister will make it through this ordeal and be well again. I just hope she doesn't have to suffer for long," answered Luise.

The nurse came looking for them to tell them Margot was out of surgery and sleeping. "There was a lot of damage to her left leg and it will take time for her to recuperate. Only time will tell if she'll be able to use it properly. She will most likely sleep through the night. Why don't you go home and come back in the morning."

"She's right, Luise, I'll take you and the baby home and I'll come back and stay with Margot," said Gerhard.

"Well, I suppose you are right. The baby should sleep in his crib tonight, but you should stay with us at home too. You need the rest," said Luise.

"I know, but I can't leave Margot all by herself at the hospital. What if she wakes up and no one is there. I'll walk you home and then I'll come back. Let's get started while it is still light." He put an arm around Luise and they headed home.

"This has been a day I hope never to see again," said Luise. "I didn't know what hell was until today. I don't know what I'll do when you go back to fight again."

"My leave is almost over and we haven't had much time together. After Margot gets better and she is able to go back home, I want you to go also and stay with your mother for a while. It's safer in Furth im Wald away from the city. I've already talked to Hans about it. He'll help you since I can't be here."

They walked through the war torn streets back to their apartment. Luise packed some food for Gerhard to take back to the hospital. She kissed him goodbye, "I love you my handsome husband. I'll miss you tonight, but I know you have to go back to the hospital. It's hard not to be selfish when I know you only have a few days left of your leave. I don't want you to go back to war. I can't help it. I'm so afraid of losing you. I want us to spend every minute together."

"I understand, my treasure, I feel the same way. I wish we could just go back to our happy life together before all this gloomy, heart sickening ruthlessness. I am ashamed and grief-stricken. I feel so helpless I could die. I'm sorry I have to leave now, but tomorrow begins a new day and we must hold on to our love," said Gerhard. He caressed her tenderly and kissed the tears trickling down her cheek.

Luise hugged him so tightly. "Be careful. You'll squish little Gunther," said Gerhard.

GETTING TO FURTH
IM WALD

Hans roamed the streets looking for some way to get to Furth im Wald. Maybe a loose horse or even a cow or bicycle. Everything was damaged or broken even Gerhard's bicycle had a flat tire with a big hole in it.

"What can I do? I can't give up," thought Hans as he stopped to rest. He leaned back against the fragment of what used to be a wall to an apartment house and closed his eyes. As he started to doze off, he was startled by the sound of an engine. He opened his eyes and peeked around the corner. To his amazement, he saw a motorcycle with a sidecar attached. He stayed very quiet and waited. The soldiers were standing nearby, so he had to be patient. He had to pick the right moment to steal the motorcycle without being shot. He watched the soldiers get back on and drive to the next block. He saw them get off and walk inside a partially standing building. Here was his chance. Was he brave enough? He stood still for a minute and took a deep breath. If he hesitated too long, he would lose any chance of stealing that motorcycle. He had nothing left to loose except his life which meant nothing to him now. Quietly he ran up to it. He mustered all his 80 year old strength and carefully pushed the 400 pound motorcycle down the street and around the corner. He stopped to rest nearly out of breath. He examined the vehicle. It was a BMW R12. It had an MG 34 machine gun attached to the sidecar and two little metal saddle bags on each side of the back wheels. He was glad to see a gas can near the front wheel in between the sidecar and motorcycle. Underneath the spare tire in back of the sidecar was a small storage compartment. It had a slightly elevated seat in back of the main motorcycle. He climbed on the seat and turned the key. He pushed down on the kickstarter, put on the green helmet and goggles and slowly started to move.

If he could average about 60 mph, he could get to Furth im Wald in about five hours. He couldn't use the main roads, so he headed for the fields and trees. He knew some of the back roads and woodland paths. The sun had almost set leaving an orange hue like a trail following him. He was headed southeast with a fierce determination. As darkness set in, he had no choice but to turn on the headlights. The back light was dim, but the front was too bright. Maybe the full moon would be enough. He stayed at the edge of the trees, turned off the lights and rode without the goggles. He could see just enough to keep moving along. The only thing he worried about was the noise. Any lights or movement he saw in the distance made him stop and turn off the engine. Most of the time it was nothing. Having to stop and hide in the bushes was slowing him down. He got down off the motorcycle to stretch and almost stepped on an adder snake. The snake was busy trying to catch a field mouse which jumped up and ran off as fast as it could go. Hans had to put his hand over his mouth to keep from shrieking out of fear. The snake slithered off and Hans almost laughed out loud. He had bigger matters to worry about. Soon he was on his way again riding as quickly as he could. Once he reached the edge of Furth im Wald, he had to find a place to hide the motorcycle and then walk the rest of the way. He couldn't think. Maybe he could cover it with brush. No, bad idea. He rode a little further until he saw a farmhouse with a barn. He took his chance and rode over to it and knocked on the door. He explained his ordeal and got them to agree to let him hide the motorcycle in the barn. He immediately left on foot to find Maria and Ilse. After about half an hour, he reached the apartment where they lived. Trying not to scare them, he knocked softly on the door.

"Who is there?" asked Maria. "Gerhard's friend Hans," he said. Maria opened the door and welcomed him inside. Hans explained the situation to them. After Maria gained her composure, she and Ilse packed their bags for the trip back to Cologne. Maria handed Hans some food and insisted he rest up for a while before they left. There was no time to waste, so Hans only took a 15 minute nap.

"Let's go," said Hans. "We have a bit of a hike to go on before our long ride back." They hurried out the door and made their way to the farmhouse. Hans opened the barn door and showed them his mode of transportation. Ilse was excited and Maria was a little taken back. Hans pushed the motorcycle out of the barn and shut the door. "Maria, I think you should ride in the sidecar and Ilse, you can ride in back of me," said Hans. Maria mustered up her courage and climbed in with the bags in her lap. Ilse was more adventurous and gladly jumped on the back while Hans was filling up the gas tank from the spare supply. He started the engine and off they rode into the gloomy night. Ilse was having fun, but Hans and Maria were aware of the danger that could lie ahead. There was no fun in it for them only uneasy feelings. Hans had no choice but to ride like the wind for when the sun comes up they will have to ditch the motorcycle and finish their trip on foot. Through the mist and darkness Hans drove as fast as the motorcycle would go. He was dauntless even when the motorcycle tipped bringing the sidecar off the ground.

Dawn was drawing near. The early morning sun broke through the gray clouds. A stream of luminous sunlight faintly glowed through the narrow gap of open sky. They had another hour's drive, but it was not safe to ride the stolen motorcycle any longer. Hans stopped and helped Maria out of the sidecar. A bit shaken, Maria exclaimed, "I'm glad that ride is over. My heart almost stopped a couple of times especially when we almost hit a tree."

"When we hit that big bump, I thought I was going to fly right off," said Ilse.

"I'm glad you were holding on tight because I almost left the seat myself," said Hans. He picked up Ilse's suitcase, held her hand and took a deep breath. "I think we should all find a place to take a short respite, but let's get clear of the motorcycle first."

Maria grabbed Ilse's other hand and they continued on their journey. They headed for the small dirt road up ahead. "My energy is getting drained," said Hans. "My feet feel like lead. Let's rest by that big tree down the road a bit."

"Sure, the motorcycle is out of sight and we need some sleep," agreed Maria.

When they reached the tree, Maria set her suitcase on the ground for Hans to use as a pillow. Ilse and Maria plopped on the ground beside him. Soon after they closed their eyes, the sounds of the soft wind blowing and the birds singing their early morning songs put them right to sleep. They were awakened about an hour later by a little squealing noise. "Don't move Ilse," said Maria. "It's just a mother skunk with her babies. We don't want to upset them. They are just curious about us." Ilse barely moved her eyes as she waited for the little skunk family to move on down the road.

"That was close. For a second I thought we were going to be smelly targets," laughed Hans. "We need to start moving again."

They started walking in the direction toward Cologne. Large dark clouds began to gather overhead releasing cold drops of rain on top of their heads. Maria and Hans ran under the nearest tree hoping to get some relief from the unexpected drench. Ilse had other ideas though. She lifted both arms out and started twirling in circles. She stuck out her tongue to catch the raindrops. "Ilse, come over here. You are getting soaking wet. Watch out for the horse and wagon!" yelled Maria. Ilse turned around just as the horse was pulled to a stop in front of her. The wagon was full of fresh hay. The driver offered them a ride as far as he was going. They gladly climbed on board. Maria sat next to the driver and Hans and Ilse rode on top of the hay. "Be careful up there," demanded Maria. "I don't want to see you rolling on the side of the road."

There wasn't much protection from the rain, but they were traveling toward Cologne and that is what mattered now. The road was bumpy, but compared to their previous ride, it was easy going. They slept on and off until the wagon stopped. " This is as far as I can take you. Cologne is about 10 kilometers straight ahead. I wish you all the best of luck. I can offer you a drink of water and a piece of bread. Stay cautious and alert. I wish I could bring you further, but I need to deliver this hay as soon as possible."

"You have been so kind and helpful. How could we ask for more?" replied Hans. "We are so close now. We will be fine." With renewed energy, they resumed their walk. The sun was a welcome sight as it peaked out from behind the clouds. Their soaked clothes had a chance to dry as they hurried along trying to avoid the muddy brown puddles.

"I wish I had as much energy as a 14 year old," said Hans as he watched Ilse skipping head. "Don't get too far ahead of us."

"The closer we get to Cologne the more dreadful I feel about my little girl. Every once in a while I feel my heart fluttering with fear. How am I going to do this?" asked Maria.

"You're not alone. We will all be there for you and Margot. I can't tell you not to worry. We are all scared for her, but we have each other to lean on," answered Hans.

As they reached the top of the hill a few hours later, Cologne was finally in sight. They tried to run, but their legs would not cooperate. There was only a few kilometers to go. They pushed themselves to keep moving along. "Let's stop at Luise's apartment first. I'm so thirsty and need to sit down," said Hans.

Luise came home to put the baby in his crib for a nap. She anxiously paced the floor trying not to torment herself with her troubled thoughts of Margot and now her mother traveling so far. She opened the kitchen window in hopes of feeling some fresh air and sunshine on her face. The disappointment shone in her eyes as the stench of death and burning rubble filled her nostrils. She quickly grabbed the window to pull it shut but the view suddenly changed when she saw three familiar figures walking down the street. She wiped her eyes to take a second look. A glimmer of hope filled her soul as she recognized her mother, Ilse and Hans. She hurriedly ran out the door and down the stairs to greet them. "What a heavenly sight," she exclaimed as she hugged her mother. Luise immediately collapsed in her mother's arms and shed tears of relief.

"Go ahead and cry my child Mother is here now," sympathized Maria as she held Luise tightly and gave her a kiss on the cheek. "Let's go upstairs and you must tell me what's happening. Is Margot okay? I must get to the hospital. Is Gerhard still there?" Luise tried to calm herself as she told her mother all she knew.

"Thank God the baby was not hurt! I need to see Margot now," said Maria.

"You've hardly slept all night. Don't you want to rest a bit first?" asked Hans.

"I can't rest until I've seen my little girl. She needs her mother," explained Maria.

"If you say so," said Hans. "Let's get going then."

"Wait!" shouted Luise. "Let me get little Gunther. I'll feed him his bottle on the way to the hospital."

"Are you sure my dear?" said Maria. "Maybe you should stay

here until we get back."

"I've waited long enough, mamma," declared Luise as she ran to get the baby and his bottle.

"Ready?" said Hans as he grabbed Maria with one hand and Ilse with the other. Together they all headed for the hospital. Maria was glad to have a man's arm to hold as they hurried down the street and up the hill.

Gerhard was overjoyed when he spied them with the corner of his eye. "I've never been so glad to see anyone in my entire life. All the people I love right before my eyes," cried Gerhard with sudden unmasked emotion.

Maria took a deep breath as they walked over to Margot's bed. "My little girl my little bluebird," she whispered to herself. "Will you ever sing again?" She picked up Margot's hand and gently pressed it to her quivering lips. She slowly reached for Gerhard's strong hand and gave it a bone crushing squeeze as she reluctantly pulled the sheet away from Margot's leg with the other hand. She thought she had seen it all in this war, but the sight of her own little girl's splintered mutilated leg gave her a fearful chill that crept up her spine.

"Mamma, you're here!" yelled Margot. "My leg hurts like someone is stabbing it with a knife. I don't know if I can move it."

Maria somehow found the strength to hold back her tears and held on to Margot's hand. "I didn't mean to wake you up. Lie still. The nurse will be back with some medicine that will help the pain go away," said Maria. "I brought you some books to read and your doll. Remember how you used to sleep with it next to your pillow every night?" Maria stayed by Margot's bedside until she fell asleep. She was anxious to talk to the doctor privately, but he looked too frazzled and ragged to carry on a lucid conversation. There were so many casualties. The doctor had been working around the clock. He told Maria he would talk to her as soon as he could. She told Gerhard, Luise and Hans to go home and rest up. They reluctantly took her advice. Ilse wanted to stay with her mother and sister. They both folded their hands and asked a kind and loving God to bless poor Margot. "Make my love strong enough and make my heart big enough to have faith in your healing power," prayed Maria. "Please forgive me for doubting you. I am at your mercy as is Margot. You are the only one that can help her now."

The doctor finally arrived to talk to Maria. "I'm Dr. Schlossman," he said. "Let's step outside for a minute. I understand Margot is your daughter. Her leg is in pretty bad shape. I tried to save it, but there is no guarantee. I have done all I can. The rest is up to Margot now."

"How soon can I take her home?" asked Maria.

"I shouldn't let her go for a least a month, but I need room for all the casualties coming in," replied the doctor. "We'll see how she is doing in a couple of days. I'm going to give you some sulfur powder now before I run out and some pain medicine also. Be very careful with it. Use it sparingly. The nurse will show you how to change the bandages and take care of the wounds. I wish I could do more. I only hope her leg doesn't become infected. That will be bad news. God bless you."

Thank you doctor," said Maria. "I'll take good care of her."

GERHARD'S LEAVE IS ENDING

The next couple of days crawled by. Maria hardly left Margot's side. Hans stopped by every day and assured Maria that he would help them get back home again when Margot could leave. "Why, I'm an old hat at getting people to their destinations."

Ilse quietly stood by not knowing how to help. All she could do is read to her sister and play with her doll together. She sometimes had to walk away when Margot's started to moan with pain before the nurse could give her more medicine for it. She closed her eyes and tried to be strong and brave like her little sister.

Luise and Gerhard were getting ready to leave the apartment and walk back to the hospital. "Only a couple of days left before I have to go back to that ugly fight. Let's take a walk along the Rhine River like we used to do before the war," said Gerhard. "Somehow we'll pretend nothing has happened. Margot has your mother and sister with her. We'll go a little later to rest them."

"How can we do that?" asked Luise. "I would have to close my eyes and plug up my nose. I used to be good at pretending, but I don't know now."

"Come on we have to do something or we'll go mad," said Gerhard.

"Okay, I'll try," said Luise

Luise picked up little Gunther and held him closely. Gerhard took Luise by the hand and gently held it to his heart. They walked outside and headed for the river. They kept their eyes only on each other as they walked along the water.

"I feel guilty taking a walk by the river thinking that Margot may never be able to walk with us again," said Luise. "What if she loses her leg? What will happen?"

"We're all afraid. Sometimes things seem hopeless, but don't be sad. We must keep our faith my precious treasure," said Gerhard in a comforting voice. "Remember when we first moved into our apartment? We had no furniture only some pillows, a blanket and an old radio."

"There was plenty of room to dance that night. I remember," said Luise. "You turned on that old radio and found a love song. You got down on your knees and sang to me. I couldn't stop laughing. You stood up and grabbed my hand to kiss it and started to dance with me. Then you tripped over your own two feet and fell flat on the floor with me on top of you."

"Well, that was my attempt to be romantic. It didn't work out exactly as I had planned," said Gerhard.

"I guess not, considering we were both lying on the floor laughing our heads off," said Luise.

"Ya, but while we were on the floor we found some romance," snickered Gerhard.

"Yes we did. I think I love you even more today than yesterday, my brave soldier," said Luise. "Halt! Do you hear something? What is that sound?"

"I don't know. I heard it too," said Gerhard. "Wait a minute. There it is again. It's over there by the water. Oh my God. It's an injured dog. Looks like it's been shot in the leg. It's a Lowchen breed and all matted and dirty. I haven't seen many of that kind of dog. If it's fur is shaved just right , it looks like a tiny lion."

"Oh, the poor little animal. What is it doing lying by the edge of the water?" asked Luise. "It sounds like it's in pain. What should we do? Who could have done such an awful thing?"

"I wish I knew," said Gerhard. "Maybe it was caught in the crossfire?"

"We can't just leave it here. We have to bring it back to the apartment, Gerhard."

They both knew they couldn't just leave it lying there still alive and in pain. Gerhard bent over to pick up the dog. "Wait," said Luise handing Gerhard the baby. She cupped her hands and scooped up some water from the river and held it by the dog's mouth. It slowly stuck out its tongue and licked the water from her hands. "I think it's a girl."

"Here take the baby back. I'll take the dog," decided Gerhard.

Luise took the baby. "Be careful."

"How are you going to take care of this dog and Margot at the same time?" asked Gerhard. "You've never even had a dog."

"Well," said Luise. "My mother is here and soon we'll be going back to her roomy apartment in Furth im Wald and anyway we've got to try. I couldn't live with myself if I didn't."

Gerhard very carefully lifted the little dog off the ground and held it gently in his arms. They walked back through the chaos in the streets where many of the homeless people were leaving their destroyed homes to find another place in nearby towns. They thanked God that they still had a place to call home. They had pity for so many unfortunate people, but there were just too many and they had their own grief to deal with at the moment.

After they arrived at the apartment, Luise put the baby in his crib and gathered some old towels for the dog. Gerhard checked her leg while Luise looked for something to use as bandages.

"We'll have to clean the leg up before we wrap it," said Gerhard. "I think her bone is splintered. We'll need some kind of a splint also to help it heal right, if it heals at all."

Luise took a small thin piece of wood out of the woodpile by the stove. They managed to wrap the leg up and put a down feather pillow on the kitchen floor by the warm stove. Luise rubbed some of the dirt off its fur and gave it some food and water. All the while, the little dog hardly yipped. She seemed to know that Luise and Gerhard were trying to help her.

Luise picked up the baby, changed his diaper and sat on the couch beside Gerhard. She fed little Gunther, then put her head on her husband's shoulder to rest and relieve her burdened mind. Worn and fatigued, she fell asleep. Gerhard slowly inched his way off the couch with the baby safely in his arms. He put the baby in his crib and softly sang a lullaby until little Gunther fell asleep. He examined the dog and covered her with one of the towels. All seemed well, so he left a note on the table telling Luise he was going back to the hospital to check on Margot.

When he got to the hospital, he saw Maria dozing off in the chair and Ilse playing with the doll on the floor. Margot was tossing and turning in her sleep.

"Why don't you and Ilse go the apartment and get some restful sleep. I'll stay a while and watch over Margot," said Gerhard.

"I can't go anywhere. What if she wakes up while I'm gone?" responded Maria. "She'll expect to see me here. I just want to get her back home. The doctor said it might be possible tomorrow."

"I know. It's hard to be patient. I wish I didn't have to go back and leave all of you again. It doesn't look good for us, Maria. Hitler is always in a rage. I think he's gone mad. He'll make us fight til nothing is left. I have already lost my honor and self-respect."

I WANT TO GO HOME

Margot was in better spirits the next morning. Her leg was hurting, but not throbbing unbearably. Gerhard had stayed the night and was getting ready to go back to the apartment to see Luise and Gunther. Hans showed up with a smile on his face. "I have good news. I was able to borrow a horse and cart from a good friend of mine. As soon as Margot is well enough to move, we can take her home. It'll be a long trek, but we will stop at Stefan and Ingrid's farm the first night. They have a cow and a few chickens and dried deer meat to eat. There is a sparkling stream nearby for fresh water. Then, we'll leave before dawn the next morning."

"Oh thank Heaven! You are a gift from God, Hans," exclaimed Maria. "What if it rains? Do you have a cover for Margot?"

"Yes, my dear. I have something for the rain. We'll make Margot as comfortable as possible," added Hans. "When will the doctor let her leave? I don't know if I can hold the cart and horse very long. Someone is sure to try and steal them if I leave them alone too long."

"Here he comes now, Hans. Let's pray he says she can go today," said Maria.

"Hello little one. Did you get any sleep?" asked Dr Schlossman. "Let me have another look at you."

Maria held her hands in prayer and closed her eyes. Han's foot was rapidly tapping up and down. He watched as Dr. Schlossman lifted the cover from Margot's leg and proceeded to carefully unwrap the bandage. As the doctor examined her leg, he sincerely hoped that God heard Maria's prayers.

"I don't know," he said. "Her leg needs a lot of care. She should stay another day at least. My biggest worry is infection."

"But I was hoping we could take her home today," said Maria with great dismay. "Hans has managed to find a horse and cart for us. He'll have to stay up all night to keep a lookout and make sure no one takes it."

"I want to go home," yelled Margot. "Please let me go home."

With much trepidation, Dr Schlossman agreed to release Margot. "I'm hesitant to let her go, but I have so many people that need a bed. I will release her under your care. I'll send the nurse to answer any questions you have. I only hope it mends well. Have a safe trip. May God be with you."

Maria thanked the doctor and turned to Hans. "I'll go get Luise and say goodbye to Gerhard and then come back to get you and Margot. See you soon then," said Hans.

"We'll be here ready and waiting."

Hans drove the horse and cart through the torn up streets to the apartment. There were still people cleaning up and digging through the rubble. Hans kept the horse moving along at a steady pace. He stopped in front of the apartment and looked up at the window. He was happy to see Luise waving to him. "Get your things," yelled Hans. "We are leaving today." He stayed by the cart until Gerhard and Luise came out with their suitcases and two baskets. One contained the baby and the other contained the little dog.

"We've got an extra passenger, but she won't take up much room. I'll tell you about it a little later. I've decided to travel with you for a short while," said Gerhard as he and Luise climbed onto the cart. "Unfortunately it is time for me to go back."

When they arrived back to the hospital , Gerhard swiftly ran inside to fetch Margot, Ilse and Maria. Margot had a clean bandage on her leg and was ready to leave. She looked so helpless lying there tightly clutching her doll. They gave each other a hug and Gerhard bent over to carefully pick her up. He slowly carried her outside just as a sprinkle of rain broke through the clouds. He hurried to get Margot into the cart and out of the wet weather. As he lowered her little body into the waiting cart, Margot watched a drop of rain fall softly on her big toe. She felt a definite tingle and said to Gerhard, "Oh my God, I just felt a teardrop from Heaven. I just know it was sent from my father to let me know he is with me. Now I know I will be all right. Daddy is praying for me."

"Yes, Margot, we all are praying for you. Remember that," replied Gerhard. "Let's get you covered up so your leg doesn't get wet."

"Here is your sister with a special surprise," said Hans.

"We've added a new member to our family," said Luise as she handed the little Lowchen dog to Margot. We'll explain later. What do you want to call her?"

"Oh my goodness! I've never seen such a precious little animal," exclaimed Margot. "Let me think. Well, I'll call her Angel because she is the little angel that daddy must have sent to keep me company and help me." She held little Angel in her arms and kissed her on the nose. Angel responded by licking Margot's face.

Luise, Gerhard and Ilse climbed in the back with Margot. Ilse sat with her legs hanging over the back while Maria and Hans sat in front. Hans motioned the horse to start moving down the road.

"Do you have all the medicine and extra bandages, mamma?" asked Luise. "I hope we didn't forget anything."

"All is well my child. We have everything with us," answered Maria.

The road was quite bumpy, but Margot remained brave. The

light rain soon stopped falling. Even miles away a few ashes still swirled about in all directions. Sometimes the road was hard to follow. Not everything was cleaned up and debris including even body parts were on the road. Hans tried to miss the crushed head on the side of the road, but it was hard to maneuver the wagon around it all. As they traveled further from the city, the cleaner air was easier to breath. They reached a small shallow stream and had to cross through it because the bridge was destroyed. It gave them all a chance to stop and stretch their legs. Gerhard carried Margot and Angel to a grassy spot. Hans let the horse drink and Luise fed baby Gunther. The serenity of the countryside was like a tranquilizer. It made them feel calm and peaceful. They had a long way to go and wanted to keep moving so it was a short respite. Soon they were on their way again. Margot slept most of the way with Angel right beside her. The sunset was radiating bright orange-red colors in the evening sky as they neared the farm. By the time they ended their day long journey, the sky was clear and the stars were twinkling.

"Look up at the sky and make a wish, Margot," said Gerhard as he picked her up in his arms. "Hold Angel tightly."

Margot didn't know which wish to choose. She wanted the war to be over. She wanted all of her family to stay safe. She wanted her leg to get better so she could walk again. She also wanted her little angel dog to be healed and run again. "I don't know."

"This wish should be something just for yourself this time," said Gerhard.

"Then I wish that Angel and I can someday run in the woods together," said Margot.

The front door opened to a smiling face. "We are so happy to see you. My name is Ingrid and this is my husband, Stefan. Hans has told us all about you. It's getting late and we were a bit worried about all of you. Won't you come inside. We have a bed ready for Margot and her mother in the second bedroom. There are extra comforters and blankets also if the rest of you want to stay on the floor in the same room.

"That's very kind of you," replied Luise in a soft grateful voice.

"I'll take a blanket to the barn," insisted Hans.

"Well, there are two families sharing the barn at the moment," said Stefan. "Some of our neighbors were not as lucky as we were."

"Oh my, did we take someone's room from them?" asked Luise.

"No, my dear. It's yours for as long as you need it," said Stefan. "You must be hungry. Ingrid is stirring the venison stew as we speak. She wanted you to have a warm meal before you get ready for bed. We've been so blessed here on our farm. We have one cow left for milk and a small vegetable garden that nobody has come to raid. We are honored to share it with you."

They all devoured the food. Margot was overjoyed to have real milk to drink. She shared some of her food with Angel. After dinner Gerhard went outside to take care of the horse. He then helped Maria bring Margot and Angel to the bed. There was just enough room for Maria to slide in beside Margot. She held her little daughter tightly and sang a sweet lullaby in her ear until she fell asleep. Luise spread out a comforter on the floor and fed little Gunther. Ingrid gave her extra rags for a change of diapers.

Hans and Stefan sat on the porch and enjoyed the cool night air. The rumbling they heard from far away caused them to take notice. They hoped it was only thunder. "What can I do to help you in the morning?" asked Hans. "You have been overly gracious. I don't know if I'll ever be able to make it up to you. Let me help you with the animals in the morning before we leave."

"My dear friend, there is no need to make it up to me. There is a war going on out there and helping you is the least I can do.

I'm just glad I am able to do something. So many people have lost everything. One of the families in my barn have no other place to go right now. I have been blessed and now I need to share what I can," said Stefan. "You have a long trip tomorrow and need to go as soon as possible."

"Your heart is in the right place, Stefan. I pray you and Ingrid stay safe," said Hans.

"Oh before I forget. Here is a pistol in case you need it," added Stefan.

"No need. I have one, the one I used to kill the bastard who shot my wife. Believe me, I know how to use it," replied Hans. "Gerda and I could have had a few more good years together. She was 79, but in good health. I hope the damn coward is burning in hell fire. Can you imagine trying to rape a seventy-nine year old woman? He caught us by surprise. I was next door helping my neighbor when I heard her scream. I pulled out my pistol which I always kept with me, and ran to the house. Right in the middle of the kitchen I saw the Russian soldier ripping Gerda's clothes off her little trembling body. I aimed and shot at him. My hand was so shaky that I don't even know if I hit him. He turned, pulled out his gun and shot Gerda point blank in the stomach. I shot two more times and he fell to the floor. I ran to Gerda, my wife of 55 years and held her in my arms. We had a last kiss before she died. Our goal was to make it at least 60 years together. I didn't think I was capable of hating anyone so deeply as I did that soldier. I hope that he rots in hell."

"What did you do with his body?" asked Stefan.

"I dragged it as far into the woods as I could and buried it. I thought of leaving it for the animals to eat, but I didn't want the animals to eat such poison," answered Hans breaking down in tears. "I managed to have a small service for my Gerda at the family cemetery. I wish there had been time to stop on the way to visit her grave, but I can go by on the way back to Cologne. I'll be staying in Luise and Gerhard's apartment for a while."

"I'm so sorry Hans," said Stefan. "I know it hurts to lose someone you love. Ingrid and I walked around senseless for weeks after we found out our son, Karl, was killed in action. We didn't know if it was day or night. A first we were just plain numb. Then we wondered if there was a God. How could he let all this happen to us? We lost our only son. He wasn't suppose to die before we did. We became so angry that we cursed everything until our throats were raw. I don't know when we came to our senses. I think it was when we finally realized that it wasn't really God that killed our son. It was a war inspired by the Devil himself for only the Devil could cause such evil to come forth on the earth. And Hitler conspired with him to gain unlimited power and cause dreadful destruction to our precious world with his prejudice and hate. But the Devil won't win. We can't let Hitler take over the world. Every day Ingrid and I pray on our knees and ask God to help our fragile world be free of all the evil that has been unleashed."

"Oh Stefan," sobbed Hans. "We all have our grievous stories to tell and burdens to bear."

"My only consolation is that Gerda doesn't have to live in this hell of a place any longer and now I can't wait to join her. What have I got left to live for?"

"If it wasn't for Ingrid, I'd feel the same way. She gives me hope," said Stefan. "Besides, I expect to see you on your way back through."

"I'm sorry for being so morbid. I think it's time for us to get some sleep. Good night my friend," said Hans. "Thanks."

Not wanting to wake anyone, Hans quietly laid on the couch to sleep for the night. His mind was racing, but his body was exhausted. It didn't take long for him to fall asleep. His nightmares were the same as he tossed and turned most of the night. It was almost a relief when morning came and he was busy getting things ready to continue their journey. He opened the door to the second bedroom and woke up Gerhard first. When all was in order, they aroused the others. Ingrid had already packed some food for them and was bringing it to the wagon. It was an hour before the morning sunrise. They were right on time and all seemed well. Everyone was on board and they were ready to head out.

"Here is some milk for the baby and some more clean rags," said Ingrid. "We wish you a safe trip back to your home."

Luise smiled at Ingrid. "We wish you all the blessings God can give for all the good you are doing for us and the others you've helped through this painful time."

The young horse had no trouble pulling the heavy cart with everyone on board. A few stars were still sparkling in the sky before darkness gave way to the light. They watched the stunning sunrise forming like a giant painting right before their eyes. Then as suddenly as it came it was gone again when the sun's bright glow peaked over the horizon with its overpowering brightness.

They traveled on for a few more hours before they stopped to rest. Gerhard turned to Luise and slowly lifted his hand to touch her cheek. "I want to look at you one last time before I must leave you." He gave her a long kiss to say goodbye before they parted ways. "This war will be over before you know it my treasure. I'll be back home again," he shouted, as he headed back to war.

Luise watched him walk away. She could not stop herself from crying. Maria put her arms around Luise knowing how hard it was to let go of the best thing that ever happened in her life. Hans was at a loss for words for he also knew that pain. All he could do was hand her a handkerchief.

"Let's keep moving," said Hans as he motioned the horse. "Every step brings us closer and nothing can stop us."

The sun was beating down on them so Maria and Luise propped up a blanket over Margot and Angel. Maria noticed the blood coming through Margot's bandage. She carefully unwrapped it. She only took a quick look at Margot's leg before she wrapped it back up. She couldn't bear to see her little girl fighting for her life.

"Her leg will heal and all will be well," she thought. But the fear made her doubt it all and she wanted to cry.

MARGOT IS
BACK HOME

"Oh Luise, what am I going to do? I am really worried. Margot's leg is so red and swollen. We better fetch Dr. Eisenhof," said Maria.

"I'll go right away," responded Luise. She ran out the door and headed down the street. She ran up the long hill until she reached Dr. Eisenhof's office. As soon as he heard red and swollen, he grabbed his bag and headed out the door with Luise.

"I have no more antibiotics left," he told Luise. "We have to use an old fashioned means of fighting the infection. Do you have any onions or garlic?"

"No, we didn't plant a garden this year, but if wild onions will work, we can find some in the woods," said Luise.

"Great, we'll search for some on the way to the apartment. Let's head for the woods," said Dr Eisenhof.

"Oh, also, our friend Jutta, grows garlic in her garden. We can ask her for some," added Luise.

After gathering the wild onions and stopping at Jutta's place, they were on their way to see Margot. Maria was waiting in the doorway. "Good," she said. "You're finally here. I'm frightened for Margot. Her leg looks bad."

"I am out of antibiotics so we had to stop at the edge of the woods to find some wild onions to make a poultice," said Dr Eisenhof. "I am hoping it will draw out the infection. I need you to cut up some cloth in large squares and heat them in some boiling water. We'll chop up the onions and place them in between the hot cloths and lay them on Margot's leg. Then crush some of the garlic and add it to a soup for Margot to eat."

When all was ready, the doctor brought the poultice over to the bed. "Hi Margot. We made something to put on your leg. We hope it will pull out some of the bad infection. I am so sorry that it will hurt a lot at first, but it will get better after it starts working. Scream if you need to. We have to do something to make your leg get better. We don't want you to lose it." He placed the poultice on her leg and Margot gave out a yelp. Her eyes filled with tears as she tightened her grip on her mother's hand.

"Why does it have to hurt so much?" she asked.

"It saddens me that you have to go through so much pain my poor little girl," said Maria. "Mamma is here. Squeeze my hand and yell as loud as you want."

Margot's sharp cry alarmed little Angel who was lying beside her. Maria caught the little dog just before she almost jumped off the bed.

"I'll be by some time late tomorrow," said the doctor. "If her leg doesn't look any better, we may have to talk about other options. Remember to change the poultice every four hours during the next 24 hours. Here is what I have left of pain medicine. Be careful to use it sparingly. I don't know when I will get any more. God bless."

"Thank you Dr. Eisenhof," said Maria. "We need all the blessings we can get."

Luise walked him to the door and waved goodbye. She brought Maria a chair so she could sit by Margot's bedside. A few hours later she heated some squares of cloth and put fresh raw onions in between them. Maria and Luise removed the cold poultice and placed the fresh one on Margot's still swollen leg as gently as they could.

"Mamma! It hurts so much. Mamma, I feel like throwing up," cried Margot as she suddenly sat up and rejected all she had from her stomach onto the floor.

"Quickly, grab the basin, Luise," yelled Maria.

Margot continued to gag and dry heave until her strength gave out and she felt lightheaded. She made a low-pitched murmur and fell back with a swift motion. Angel yipped and almost fell off the bed again.

"Margot," shouted Maria. "Are you okay?"

"I think she has fainted," said Luise.

"Check her breath. Do you feel anything?" Maria asked in a panicked voice.

"Mamma, calm down. I can feel her breath. Here put your hand near her mouth," declared Luise. "At least she has some relief from the pain."

"How can you be so calm, Luise? Your sister could die or lose her leg. I'm frightened. I haven't had such a sick feeling since the day your father died. I don't think I can survive another death. I can't. I just can't," shouted Maria.

"Mamma, I carry fear with me every day. I'm scared to death my Gerhard will die. I'm scared for Margot. What will happen to my child in all this? I'm scared to be alone during a war never knowing if anyone of us will get blown up or shot or raped. Do you think I look forward to getting up in the morning knowing that men have spread a disease on the earth called war. And yes. I'm sick and tired of it and I feel helpless."

"Oh my child, I'm sorry for my moment of weakness. I can't let Margot see me like this. I'm going to wash my face," said Maria.

"Mamma, why don't you lay down for a while and rest. I'll sit by Margot. If she wakes up, you'll be close by," said Luise.

"Okay, I need some rest. Wake me in half an hour."

Luise let Maria sleep as she continued to change the poultice. She managed to keep little Gunther quiet in the other room. She and Ilse made him paper airplanes and sock puppets to play with. After supper he finally fell asleep with his homemade toys and Ilse beside him.

With everyone asleep, Luise walked out onto the porch. A neighbor was walking by and stopped to talk.

"Hello Luise," called out Ute. "You couldn't sleep either? How is little Margot doing?"

"The swelling in her leg has gone down a bit. I'm letting everyone sleep," answered Luise. "Come sit with me."

"I have some chamomile I picked yesterday. I'll bring some for Margot in the morning. It should be dry by then to make a tea." said Ute.

"Okay, thanks," said Luise. "How much longer can this war last? There is not much of Germany left standing."

"Now not only the Gestapo are arresting and killing anyone that gets in Hitler's way, the SS are doing horrid things," whispered Ute. "Some people are wondering what's really happening to all the people that are taken away. I heard stories about the work camps and concentration camps that they don't have enough food to eat and are being worked to death. The SS were originally formed to be Hitler's protection squad who pledged obedience unto death. Well, it seems obedience means not only killing the men, but women even pregnant women and babies. How can anyone do that? Even if it is the enemy."

"I know they hide so much from us, but this? Gerhard never

mentions anything about the war when he writes," said Luise. "I know my love. He could never be a part of anything like that."

"I'm sure you are right, Luise," said Ute. "Gerhard is not an SS soldier and not everyone wants to follow Hitler. The older people are not convinced, but Hitler eliminates any opposition and finds ways to control not only the men and women, but the children. He gets a hold on the the children as soon as they are born. Thousands of young women are being praised for having the so-called pure master race babies in the breeding program. They are all taught to worship and pray to Hitler. He is conditioning their innocent minds!"

"It's all wrong," exclaimed Luise. "I want my child to have a mind of his own and to be able to express his individuality. Gerhard will know what to do. When he comes home Gunther and I will be safe again."

LITTLE ANGEL

Morning came too soon. Luise hardly slept, but her diligence with Margot's poultice paid off. Margot looked relieved and was smiling. The redness and swelling were noticeably subsiding.

"How do you feel today?" asked Maria.

"My leg only hurts a little now, but Angel's leg is swollen this morning. Will you look at it, mamma?" asked Margot.

"Oh my, she is not looking good. Do we have anything left for a poultice? I'll look and see if I can fix one for her," said Maria.

"I've been rubbing her leg every day. I thought her leg was better," said Margot.

"I've been paying so much attention to you, I've neglected poor Angel," said Maria.

"We'll have Dr Eisenhof look at her when he comes to see you today," said Luise. She picked up Angel from Margot's bed and carried her outside. "She can hardly stand up. Her leg must really hurt. You poor little dog. You've been so sweet. I hope you get well." Angel slowly walked out to a sunny spot and with a slight whimper laid down. Luise brought out an old towel for her to rest on.

Maria was heating up some mushroom soup for breakfast and the chamomile tea that Ute brought for Margot. "Later, we'll go to the woods and look for berries and peppermint," she said to Luise who had just come inside.

"Look who I found outside," said Luise.

"Good morning," said Dr Eisenhof. "How is our girl?"

"She is doing so much better, but our dog is not looking so well. Can you look at her please?" asked Luise. "I know you are not a vet, but you know more than we do."

The doctor turned toward Luise and scratched his head. "I suppose I can. I've been asked to do worse." After the doctor checked Margot, he grabbed his bag and walked outside with Luise. Angel was lying on the ground where Luise left her. Her tail wagged when she saw them come toward her. The doctor looked her over and listened with his stethoscope. "Angel is such a pretty dog. Her leg is a little swollen and is getting infected, but her biggest problem seems to be her heart. I don't like the sound of it. It is beating erratically and her breathing is labored. It sounds like she has a bad heart. I'm more worried about that than her leg right now."

"What do you mean?" asked Luise.

"A possible heart attack in the near future I'm afraid," said the doctor. "Make a poultice for her leg and let her rest."

"So you are telling me she will never run with Margot one day. Now my heart feels broken," said Luise. "Margot is so attached to that dog. We all love the dog."

"We've got to let Margot know about the dog. She needs time to prepare herself for the inevitable. Don't you think?" asked Dr Eisenhof.

"Yes doctor. I know," said Luise.

They walked back inside with Angel wobbling behind.

"Dr Eisenhof, how is my Angel?" asked Margot.

The doctor looked at Luise with a sad, half smile, then walked over to Margot. "Angel has been a good companion for you and a friend. Hasn't she?" said the doctor. " Dogs like Angel are very special.   They have the ability to make us happy. But they are only here for a short time. They don't live as long as people do. Angel is sick and I can't tell you how much longer she has left so don't waste your time being sad or crying. Let each moment be precious like a cherished gift. Let Angel know how much you love her and how glad you are to have her next to you. That will make her happy."

"Thank you, Dr Eisenhof, for your help," said Maria. She picked up Angel and put her beside Margot.

"We're going to put a poultice on your leg," said Margot. "You'll be all better soon and we'll be happy again."

The next few days seemed to drag by as Margot laid in bed watching everyone around her busily moving about. She could not help feeling jealous. She wanted to go outside and play or do something besides wasting away in her bed. At least she had Angel to hold and talk to. She rubbed Angel's leg and kissed her cheek. "Today I am going to try out my crutches," she said to Angel. "Soon you will be joining me and we will be hiking up to the top of Hohen Bogen where I used to sing and yodel." But Angel did not answer with her usual bark or lick on the face.

"What's wrong with Angel?" asked Ilse. "She's not breathing right. Should we get the doctor?"

"Oh no! My little Angel come here," said Margot as she cradled Angel in her arms and sang softly in her ear. She cupped her hands around the little dog's face and softly said, " I love you my precious one." Their eyes met. Margot saw the fear and confusion in Angel's eyes. Angel clenched her teeth tightly together and gave a little whimper. Then she took her last breath and died in Margot's arms. Margot's hands started shaking. She felt a stinging pain in her chest like a knife pushing through her heart leaving a gaping hole.

" I want to go with her. I don't want to live without her," uttered Margot. "Why does everything I love have to die? Maybe I didn't rub her leg good enough. My little Angel, didn't I love you enough? I can't lose you." Margot kissed Angel's cheek and just cried.

"Daddy will take care of Angel for you in heaven," sympathized Ilse. She sat on the bed and put her arms around them.

When Margot was ready, they wrapped Angel in a blanket and took her outside for a memorial. Luise carried Margot to the spot where Angel would be buried. Maria had already dug a deep hole and Ilse gathered some wild flowers. Together they carefully lowered Angel down into the ground. Margot felt almost numb as she threw the flowers into the grave with a blank look on her face.

As the days went by, Margot's depression got worse. She didn't care if she lived or died. She couldn't find solace or the will to live. Ilse tried to help her sister by reading her stories and holding her while she cried. It was hard for Ilse to hold back her own tears for she loved little Angel too. She tried to help Margot stand up, but her injured leg would give way. With the help of Maria and Luise they finally managed to get her out of bed to eat some soup.

"How long can this go on?" asked Maria. "I can't stand to see her like this."

"Give her time," replied Luise. "A heart that is broken is a painful ordeal to live through. She has two injuries to cope with now."

THE END OF DESTRUCTION

By the end of WWII in May of 1945, the Third Reich was in ruins. Hitler and his followers left destruction and shocking devastation in their wake. The large numbers of deaths worldwide can only be estimated at 55 million. Whole cities were destroyed leaving millions of people with no hope and no place to go. The concentration camps were an unbelievable sight with not only starving and sick people, but dead left unburied. Bergen-Belsen camp was burned down because many people had typhus.

The United States was pulled into the war on December 8, 1941, the day after Japan's air strike on Pearl Harbor. That same day, Hitler ordered the German Navy to attack US warships on sight and on December 11, Germany declared war on the US.

Because Germany invaded the Soviet Union in June 1941 in direct violation of the German-Soviet pact, the Soviet Union became an ally to the United States and Britain.

War was being fought in numerous fronts such as the war in the Pacific with Japan, the war in North Africa and the war in Europe. It wasn't until September 11, 1944 that the American troops entered Germany. On May 2, 1945 the German military in Berlin surrendered to the Soviets and in the West on May 7 and the East on May 9. The day the war was proclaimed finally over was May 8, 1945. Hitler committed suicide in his underground bunker in Berlin on April 30, 1945.

GERHARD HEADS HOME

Gerhard and Heinz, his army comrade, found themselves in a muddy, foul smelling hole that they had dug waiting for the enemy who were closing in fast.

I'm tired of all this killing. My heart has never been in it. This is so meaningless. I'm nothing more than a coward for going on with all this injustice. I'd like to look Hitler straight in his eyes and tell him just what I think of him and then put my hands around his neck. What a damn fool I am," whispered Gerhard to Heinz.

"Shut up, Gerhard, before someone hears you," said Heinz. "This is not the time or place for such carryings on. Pick up your rifle, aim and shoot."

To save his own life, Gerhard reluctantly held his rifle and prepared to shoot. He was not a coward. He just didn't believe in what he was doing anymore. He had lost count of how many enemies he had killed long ago. He started shooting, but there was no use trying to hold them back. They just kept coming and coming. Gerhard and Heinz had no choice but to retreat. They climbed out of the putrid hole and ran behind a large pine tree. The enemy was a short distance away, so they had to run further back into the woods. Gerhard lost sight of Heinz, but the bullets were too close to flounder. He thought he heard one pass by his ear which meant his legs needed to move faster than ever. Run! Run! Run! The resounding boom was much too close. He ducked as a tree was blown apart, pieces of wood soaring through the air. It brought back a flood of memories about his little Margot and her injured leg. Then someone screamed to his left and a shriek came from behind. Should he stop to help? He couldn't think clearly. The noise was blasting in his ears and his head was about to explode. His adrenaline kept his legs moving until his body finally gave up. He had to stop for a moment. Ahead he saw a soldier lying on the ground. He heard a muffled voice and walked toward him. He saw blood gushing out of his missing arm and felt a sudden pang of anguish through his body. He bent down to his knees with genuine sympathy and tried to stop the bleeding. He tore off a piece of his own shirt and covered what was left of the severed arm. His attempt to stop the bleeding was futile. He looked into the wounded soldier's empty eyes and watched him die. Gerhard suddenly released his bottled up emotions and began to cry. He leaned over the lifeless body and closed the motionless eyes. He was crushed as he looked around and saw that most of his army buddies were dead or dying all around him. How did this happen? What kind of world was he living in? It had turned into a nightmare. He was ready to give up. He couldn't move. He was too tired and completely ashamed of himself. He looked up and cried out for forgiveness. He felt the warm tears flowing down his cheek and his heart bleeding inside his pounding chest. The shooting stopped. Everything was quiet now except for an occasional moan heard in the distance. He was at a loss and overwhelmed. He sat on the ground and closed his eyes. He felt a wave of melancholy enter his perplexed, shattered mind. Just then he heard someone running from behind and was ready with his rifle. He didn't really want to die today, so he turned to shoot. His arms were a little shaky, but he could manage to do what was necessary to keep alive. As the form came into view, he was relieved to see Heinz running toward him with his arms waving wildly in the air.

"The war is over!" screamed Heinz, "Berlin has been captured!

The Fuhrer is dead! He has taken the cowards way out while we were out here fighting a losing battle."

"What do you mean?" asked Gerhard.

"Word has it that Hitler committed suicide," explained Heinz. "Look we are close enough to home. Let's start walking back. Hitler's gone and his German army has surrendered. Why do we have to kill anymore? Let's just drop our weapons and go home to our families. You still have a wife and a little son you hardly know."

"You couldn't be more right, Heinz," said Gerhard as he let his rifle slip out of his hand and onto the ground. "The trek home will take us about two days I would guess."

"So let's get moving. We have about six hours of daylight left," announced Heinz.

They walked and walked until they were weary and exhausted. "Let's take a break and rest a while. My boots are so worn they are almost falling off my feet," said Heinz.

"I never asked you," said Gerhard. "What did you do before the war?"

"I wanted to become a lawyer. I wanted to defend the innocent and work for justice and rights for everyone. I wanted to help my people, my country," said Heinz. "It was all pulled out from under me before I could even finish school. What happened to justice?"

"You had to follow orders just like I did," said Gerhard.

"Did I?" asked Heinz.

"If you wanted to live and come back to your family, you had to follow orders. When all this is over maybe you can go back to school," said Gerhard.

"After all the orders we had to follow. After all we destroyed and all the lives we've taken from this earth, how could I?" asked Heinz. "The war has changed us all. We have been deceived and raped by our own government. We have no freedom and very few choices. I am a fool and I have no right to stand up for others. Needless to say, my heart is not in it as it was before the war. I am an immoral person, no better than an animal. Instead of practicing law, I would be practicing deceit!"

"Don't be so hard on yourself," said Gerhard. "I know how you feel, but once you get home, you'll feel better. Hey look. There's a small farmhouse up ahead. Maybe they'll let us sleep in their barn tonight or be kind enough to give us something to eat. I'm so hungry I'd be happy to chew on an old bone. Let's think of getting home and stop feeling sorry for ourselves. We cannot change the past, but the future is not yet written."

"You're right my friend. Let's head over to the farmhouse," said Heinz.

They mustered enough energy to walk to the farmhouse and knock on the door. They were greeted by an old couple who invited them in. When the door was opened the first thing that they noticed was a large cuckoo clock hanging on the wall with a pair of antlers on each side. Underneath was a bench obviously handmade by the farmer. As they stepped in and looked around, they were surprised to see two SS soldiers sitting at the dinner table. It looked like they had been drinking so Heinz and Gerhard turned to leave.

"Where are you going? Come sit down," insisted the first soldier. "You don't want to be rude do you? What's your name soldier?"

"I'm Heinz and he is Gerhard. We're not planning to stay long," said Heinz as he pulled up a chair.

"Did you loose your rifles or did you leave them outside?" said the second soldier.

"They look like deserters to me," said the first soldier.

"Hey, maybe you're right. Something looks wrong," said the second soldier.

"Don't you know the war is over," yelled Heinz, "and the Fuhrer is dead."

"Well now, aren't we full of information today," said the first soldier as he stood up.

"All we want to do is go back to our homes to see what is left of our families," said Gerhard with tears running down his face.

"Well, come outside and I'll show you the way home," said the first soldier.

"No!" exclaimed the old woman. But she was shoved out of the way as the two soldiers pulled Heinz and Gerhard out of their chairs in order to drag them outside.

"I don't like to repeat myself, we are going outside," stated the first soldier again as they pulled Gerhard and Heinz outside and stood them side by side.

"Why are you doing this," said the old farmer. "The war is over and it's hopeless to try and fight any more."

"We are not allowed to give up. The Fuhrer says that life never forgives weakness and he forbids us to ever surrender. Deserters must be shot."

"You can't just shoot them," said the farmer.

"Who's going to stop me?" said the first SS soldier.

The farmer and his wife, not ready to die yet, went back inside. Heinz and Gerhard were trapped. If they turned to run, the bullets would surely bite them in the back, so they chose to face their destiny bravely. It all seemed like slow motion. As the German SS lifted their rifles to shoot, Gerhard had just enough time to quickly fasten two buttons on his jacket. He looked at the SS straight in the eyes as they were ready to pull the trigger. His whole life's memories flashed before his eyes. It was then that he knew who his enemy really was. Six shots were fired and he fell to the ground in a pool of blood.

LUISE WANTS TO GO BACK TO COLOGNE

When Luise heard the war was over she somehow had to make her way back to Cologne. She just wanted to be home at her apartment when he arrived. She knew that she was taking a big risk. Maybe her apartment was gone. She hadn't heard from Hans in a while. She knew her precious Gerhard would find her and they would be reunited again to continue their lives together. She knew things would be very different than they had planned, but they would have each other to find a way to go on with their lives. She hadn't seen him in almost three years. All she had was a few letters letting her know he was still alive.

"Mamma, I want to take little Gunther and go back to Cologne and wait for Gerhard there," said Luise.

"Oh no!" exclaimed Maria. "You should stay here with us."

"A few of the boys have already gotten home. I saw one with an army jeep," said Ilse. "Maybe he will help you. His name is Franz. He used to be our neighbor. I can go ask him."

"You can't just ask him to take me to Cologne. He'll laugh at you," said Luise.

"Not if we explain that you are waiting for your soldier to come home and that he hasn't seen his little baby for such a long time," said Ilse. "I'm sure he has a family too. He used to play his guitar and sing in the back yard. I think he kind of liked you."

"That was a long time ago. Maybe he doesn't even remember. I don't think we should bother him," said Luise.

She had barely finished her sentence when Ilse left running out the door. Luise followed her with now three year old Gunther in her arms. They timidly knocked on the door. Luise was just about to turn around when Franz opened it. He had a bandage on the left side of his face covering is eye. "Hello Luise and Ilse how you've grown," he said. "Please excuse my appearance. Come in."

"We don't want to bother you. We're glad you are home," said Luise.

"My poor sister needs to get back to Cologne to wait for her husband to return from the war. His little child doesn't even know his father," said Ilse. "Please bring her home with your jeep."

"That isn't my jeep," said Franz. "I will be returning it soon."

"But you just have to help Luise. She needs to go home and wait for Gerhard."

"I can't. If I get caught I will be in big trouble," said Franz.

"It will only take a couple of days. No one will even know you're gone," said Ilse. "You've taken chances every day. Take one more, please."

"Ilse," said Luise. "Leave Franz alone. Can't you see he has a bandage on his head. Maybe he shouldn't be traveling right now."

"I can still see out of the other eye. I'm one of lucky ones," said Franz. "Okay, I'll take the chance. I'll drive you back to Cologne."

"Are you sure you'll be alright? I'll have little Gunther with me too," said Luise.

"We'll leave early tomorrow morning. I need to get back before they notice that I am missing," said Franz.

"How can I ever thank you. I'm so grateful," cried Luise.

"Just give your Gerhard all your love and understanding," said Franz.

"I will. I will," replied Luise.

She and Ilse ran back home to tell Maria and Margot. "We've got great news. I have a way to get home. Franz is going to take Gunther and me. We leave tomorrow."

"I really wish you would stay here, but I can understand why you want to go to your own apartment. I pray you stay safe. If your apartment is not livable you can always come right back," said Maria.

"Yes, mamma, we'll be okay no matter what," said Luise. "Can you help me get everything ready for tomorrow?"

"Of course. You'll need something to use for overnight diapers. You may not be able to wash them for a while. I'll cut up some clean rags and other things for you. Remember his little potty chair for daytime. Ilse and I can help gather some food for you to bring. I'll send Ilse to the woods for mushrooms and firewood.

"I want to help too," yelled Margot from her bedroom. Her slight limp was barely noticeable and her scars were healed over.

"Help me find the old picnic basket for food and water. Also, Gunther will need some toys to bring with him," said Maria.

They kept busy until all was prepared for the trip. Luise could hardly sleep and Gunther felt the excitement around him that made him more restless than usual.

In the morning Franz knocked anxiously at their door. Everything was packed and ready. Franz loaded the jeep and Luise and Gunther climbed in. Without hesitation they were on there way to Cologne.

"We're going home," said Luise as she squeezed little Gunther's hand.

"Sing a song, mamma," replied Gunther.

LUISE WAITS FOR GERHARD'S RETURN

"It looks like the apartment is still standing," said Franz. "Let's take a look inside."

"The coast is clear," said Franz as he slowly opened the door. "Let me check it out first." He walked inside and looked around. There was a bed in the middle of the den so he walked over to the closed bedroom door and carefully opened it. He noticed the missing ceiling first. Then he scanned down with his eyes and saw the broken window and the large hole in the floor. "Luise, I'm not sure if you should stay here. The bedroom has been destroyed. The apartment may not be safe. We can rest a bit and you can come back with me."

Cautiously, Luise walked through the apartment with little Gunther in her arms. "Most of the apartment is still intact. I'll close and lock the bedroom door and Gunther and I can sleep in the den," said Luise. "It'll be big enough for the two of us. If Hans returns, we'll make room. Yes, I want to stay and wait here."

"If I can't talk you out of it, let's bring in your belongings. We can eat the food your mother fixed for us and then I need to get back to Furth im Wald," said Franz.

Luise was beside herself with excitement. "Your father will be home soon my priceless little boy. Everything will be alright now. Our lives will go back to normal and we can be happy again." Luise held Gunther and danced around the kitchen.

"I'll get the suitcases and other stuff. You just watch that little boy of yours," said Franz as he started out the door and almost bumped into Hans headfirst. "Oh, you must be the famous Hans that Luise has talked so highly of during our trip here. She told me you were a real God sent. I'm glad to see you and that you have been taking care of her apartment. Luise insisted on coming back here to wait for her husband to return.

"Yes," said Hans. "I come by every few days to make sure no one tries to take over the apartment. I was staying here to watch the place, but when a bomb destroyed part of the apartment, a friend offered me a room at his place. There is no running water. I think you came all this way for nothing."

"I don't think Luise will come back with me and I can't stay here," said Franz.

" I'll find a way for her to stay. I'll bring her a bucket of water tonight," said Hans. " Is that your jeep outside? Let me help you." The two of them brought up the suitcases and supplies for Luise and Gunther.

"Thanks. I hope you stay long enough to enjoy some of our food. It needs to be eaten anyway," said Franz.

"Yes, please stay and eat with us," said Luise as she hugged Hans. "You were always one of Gerhard's favorite teachers and you have helped us so much."

"Maybe just a little. I don't want to eat all your food. It's not the easiest thing to come by these days," said Hans.

"I have to go back to Furth im Wald tonight before they notice that I am missing. I'm sure you will be checking in on Luise often. I won't worry about her as much and her mother will be grateful," said Franz.

"Oh yes. I'll be back and forth visiting a lot," said Hans. "Luise and little Gunther will be well taken care of."

It wasn't long before Luise was all by herself with the baby. After they finished eating, Franz headed home. Then Hans went to get the promised water, dropped it off and left so Luise and Gunther could get some rest. Luise cleaned up the best she could saving as much water as possible. She pushed the bed against the wall and put Gunther down for the night. She pulled a chair by the window and stared into the night. Her memories opened to the first time she met her Gerhard when she was still innocent and naive. "Have you ever seen the sky so full of stars, Gerhard," Luise asked.

"Only twinkling in your eyes," answered Gerhard. As their eyes met it seemed they needed no words to communicate their love for each other. It was as if they had always known each other. As time went by, even during disagreements their loving affection always won and they could not stay angry at each other for very long. She was looking forward to their nightly walks along the river. Now there would be three of them. It didn't matter that Gerhard could not be there for the birth of their son. He had only seen his little child for a few short fleeting moments, but soon he would be with both of them from now on and Luise would never let him out of her sight again. She was exhausted and slipped into bed next to little Gunther.

The next morning she kept busy first looking for candles to light and leave burning in the window every night. She found a large barrel in the basement to use for collecting rain water falling from the roof. This would give her wash water for her and the baby. She wanted to look as presentable as she possibly could for her returning soldier. She could take a big pot full of the water and boil it on her wood-burning stove and even use it to drink.

The days seemed to drift by slowly as if everything were suspended in time. Hans did come by often to bring extra water and food. Luise paced the floor and kept hope in her heart. Her candles were almost gone, but she would keep one burning in the window as long as she could. Her Gerhard would be coming home any day now and that's all that mattered! Suddenly the candle in the window blew out. The loud knock on the door startled her. She jumped up out of the chair and darted to the door. "Maybe my love has finally made it home," she thought. The old warped door squeaked as she tugged to pull it open. As fast as her heart was pounding she was sure she would faint dead away. She was so nervous that her hands started to sweat and she almost lost her grip on the doorknob. "The awaited moment has arrived," she thought to herself as the door flung open. She opened her arms with anticipation, but abruptly halted in her tracks when she saw who was standing on the other side of the door. She did not recognize the old woman and the aging man. "Are you Luise Thomas?" the old woman asked. Luise nodded and stepped aside to invite them in. "We have come a long way to find you."

"I don't understand," said Luise. "Do I know you? What do you want?"

"Can we sit down?" asked the old woman.

"Please forgive me for being so rude," said Luise with an apologetic voice. "I was hoping to find my dear husband at the door. He is on his way home right now."

The old woman continued. "I'm sorry we have to meet under these circumstances my dear. We live in a village almost two days from here." By now Luise was in a panic. She wanted to run because she was afraid of what she might hear. "Please stop pacing and come sit down by us. We won't bite. We need to talk to you. Your husband Gerhard and his friend, Heinz, came to our farm a couple of weeks ago seeking shelter. It was very unfortunate for them as two SS soldiers were also there using our home for a respite. They were already drunk when they saw your husband and his friend. They immediately gave them a hard time. When your husband tried to leave, they accused him of being a deserter and I don't know how to tell you this," as the old woman cast down her head with a sigh.

Luise was speechless for she knew what kind of news they had brought with them. Her beloved Gerhard would never come home. How could she go on living? She wanted to die right then and there, but she had to think about the baby. Yes, she still had the baby.

"You look just like the picture I found in your husband's jacket. On the back was an address and name," said the old farmer as he handed it to her. "We hoped it was the information we needed to find you. Your husband had a friend with him. I remember their names were Gerhard and Heinz. They looked so worn down as they came inside our home. They tried to leave when they saw the SS, but were trapped and couldn't run. The SS showed no mercy. Your husband and his friend were not carrying any rifles so that meant desertion to the SS. They tried to reason with the SS reminding them that the war was over and all they wanted to do now was to go home to their families. But you just cannot reason with the minds of the SS soldiers. I'm sorry, but they shot your husband and his friend with no remorse. The SS made us bury their bodies. The only thing we managed to save were their jackets. The SS stayed at our farm for almost two weeks. We were scared for our lives and did what they ordered us to do. We are so deeply sorry for you. I wanted to kill both of them. I wanted to grab their rifles and shoot them with all of their own bullets. Please forgive us for being so cowardly. We are greatly ashamed of ourselves."

After a long moment of silence, Luise composed herself enough to thank them for coming to see her. "I know it wasn't easy for you to travel so far. You hold no blame. I might never have known what happened to my poor husband."

The baby started to cry, but she was too numb to move. The old woman stood up and picked up Gunther. She brought him into the kitchen and made soup for everyone with what she could find in the kitchen. Luise did not eat supper. She just sat by the window and stared into the distance.

"We'll stay the night and take care of things for you. Come here little one. Let's eat something before you go to bed," said the old woman to little Gunther. "Should I make her eat something too?"

"Just let her be," said the old man. " She seems to be staring at the sunset. She'll come around when she is ready."

"I guess you're right. She needs time to grieve. All of this has been very shocking for her. I wish I knew what to say to her."

The old couple found a blanket and slept on the floor. All was silent for the night. Early the next morning little Gunther was already running around the apartment. Luise had finally fallen asleep with her head on the windowsill clutching the half burnt candle. Hans showed up with some bread and a few eggs to make. He introduced himself. He was shaken to tears when he heard the bad news. "I live nearby. I'll take care of Luise and the baby. They are close friends of mine."

"That's good to hear," said the old woman as she picked up Gunther to change his diaper. "We need to get back to our farm. My husband and I are all alone. Poor Luise is grief-stricken right now. Maybe we should stay a few days to help."

"That's very kind, but I'll stay here with them as long as I need to. I will most likely bring them back to Furth im Wald to her mother and sisters," said Hans. "Go and take care of your own affairs. I'll help them manage things here."

The old woman walked over to Luise and hugged her. "Sorry to wake you, my dear. We wish you God's blessings. Take care of your precious baby. He needs you now. Your friend Hans is here to help take care of things. We will remember you in our prayers. I'll leave our address on the table. Maybe someday we will meet again."

Luise looked up with her eyes half open. "Thank you so much. You will be blessed for your kindness. Be careful and get home safely."

Hans gave them each a piece of bread and they were on their way. "Don't get up. Luise, I'm here now. I'll get us some breakfast."

Luise closed her eyes and sobbed. "What have they done, Gerhard? The world is insane. God is crying. The earth is crying. I'm crying. Can we ever repair it? Will we ever?"

THE AMERICANS
ARE COMING

"The Americans are coming! Ilse, hide! You are sixteen now! Go upstairs in the attic," yelled Maria. Ilse ran up the stairs before anyone could see her. She stumbled into the little closet already full of old winter clothes. She hid behind the coats and tried to breath as slowly and quietly as she could. She kept thinking, "they won't find me in here. What if they do? They will rape me and maybe even beat me. But these are Americans, not Russians. They are still the enemy, but not as evil as some of the others. Please, God, I ask just one thing. Please don't let them find me." Her heart was fluttering like a cornered wild animal. She took a deep breath and tried to listen. Everything was muffled. She couldn't make out what they were saying.

"It's just my little daughter and me," said Maria as she squeezed Margot's hand and ushered two American soldiers into the house. She could feel the sweat rolling down her face. Her back felt soaking wet. Margot did not say a word as the two American soldiers circled around them. Her leg had healed, but minor scars and thin patches of skin were still noticeable on the side of her leg. Her limp was gone.

"It's okay. We won't hurt you," said one of the soldiers in broken German. "My name is Dave and this is Johnnie." He put his hand in his pocket and pulled out a stick of gum and held it out for Margot to take. She took a step back away from the soldier and almost fell backwards. "It's not poison. It's good. You can take it. Believe me," said Dave.

Margot looked at her mother for reassurance. Then held out her hand to receive her unexpected treat. She slowly closed her hand. She felt excitement running up her spine until it reached her head and made her smile.

"Well now," said Dave, "that's what I like to see, a frown turn into a smile."

"They are not acting like our enemies," thought Margot. "Maybe the Americans are not so bad after all." She thanked Dave and smelled her gum through the wrapper.

Dave and Johnnie searched the house. Maria, of course, did not trust the enemy soldiers and followed them like a shadow. All she could think about was her sixteen year old daughter hiding from the bad men. She kept saying over and over in her mind, "please don't let them find Ilse." As the soldiers walked up the stairs to the attic, Maria started to panic. She felt her heart beat like the pounding of a drum and her legs felt weak. She held tightly to the railing as she followed them upstairs.

Dave and Johnnie took a quick look around. Then they headed for the little closet that was standing against the wall near the right hand corner of the room. Maria closed her eyes as Dave opened the door and looked in. He turned to Johnnie and said, "nothing in here but some old clothes." Then he closed the door and glanced at Maria with a slight smirk and headed out of the room. Maria's fear subsided when the two soldiers seemed satisfied. She followed them down the stairs and stood by Margot. Dave and Johnnie bid them goodbye and finally left them alone. She watched them walk down the street to follow the tanks to the next apartment house. Able to breath again, she turned toward Margot, who was still standing motionless and uttered, "They're gone. I must go upstairs and tell Ilse that it is alright to come out now."

Margot sighed, took a deep breath and sat on the couch with

the stick of gum in her hand.

"Ilse, they are gone," yelled Maria as she ran up the stairs. Ilse cracked open the door to the attic closet and carefully peaked out just in case they were holding her mother at gunpoint. She was relieved to see her mother alone as she cautiously stepped out. She started laughing out loud to cover her fear. "Mamma, is it really safe now?" asked Ilse as she gave her mother a long firm hug. "My hands are still shaking."

"Yes, my sunshine," answered Maria. "They have left and you are safe." Maria put her arm around Ilse's shoulder as they headed downstairs.

"How long was I in that closet, mamma?" asked Ilse. "It felt like hours. I thought I was gonna suffocate and when the soldier opened the door to the closet, I was so scared. I held my breath. He moved the clothes and I think he saw me."

"It wasn't that long," said Margot still sniffing the aroma of her stick of gum. "Look what I got."

"You have a stick of chewing gum?" asked Ilse with a bit of jealousy in her voice.

"Oh, I'll share it with you if you really want some," said Margot.

"It's okay," said Ilse. "You can keep it. Half a stick of gum is not enough to chew anyway."

"Here, you can smell it," said Margot as she showed it to Ilse.

"You are supposed to put it in your mouth and chew it," declared Ilse.

Margot kept the stick of chewing gum for a week. She smelled it every day, but didn't dare chew it. She was still suspicious and worried that the gum was poisoned. Temptation finally got a hold of her and forced her to surrender her fear and take the risk of gambling with her life. "At least I'll die happy," she thought.

First she sniffed it one last time. Then she unwrapped it. She held it in her hand and gave it a long steady look trying to muster enough courage to lick it.

"You've been carrying that thing with you for a week," yelled Ilse as she walked by. "Why don't you just put it in your mouth or I will."

Margot looked at her sister, stuck out her tongue and popped the gum in her mouth.

Margot's mind returned back to her present day 50 years later sitting at her kitchen table drinking her coffee. Yawning and tired she brings her empty cup to the sink. She knows her life is so much better now, but it is so hard to leave the past alone. She turns toward the bedroom to head back to bed, but she just can't shake it. As tears roll down her face, she marches to the bathroom mirror. She puts her finger on her cheek. "That's the spot Hitler kissed me," she cried. She turns on the faucet and pumps the soap in her hand. She proceeds to rub the spot with her soapy hand as if she could rub that false, misleading kiss off of her face. The memories hang on. As hard as she tried, she just couldn't remove them.

HEAVEN IS WAITING FOR YOU

We are like a drop of water rolling down a hill heading toward the larger pool. It flows through dirt and sand, but instead of getting dirty, it is cleansed and purified before it joins the larger water. We can also say we are a drop of heaven (little souls falling to earth to get purified) separated from the whole, but still a part of it. As we journey through our lives on earth, a cleansing process is taking place intended to peel off everything we are "not" such as envy, greed, anger or hate exposing and leaving only love which is our true and only nature. When we finally return to our origin, we leave behind all the things that would pollute it and we bring only the love which gives it more strength and adds to its perfection.

Our common quest is to look for and find the Love that we are truly made of. We are to become intimate with that Love. We should embrace it and let it embrace us. It should become our constant companion. We should bring it along wherever we go and leave all the other things that are not related to it behind. As we study Love, we see that it also brings along lovely things such as joy, kindness and caring. Our mutual quest is to bring back to God as much of this precious Love as we can when we leave the earth and shed our physical bodies.

Learn to love everything. See the good in everything and happiness will follow.

Walk with love, talk with love, eat with love, think with love, pray with love etc. etc. and ultimately die with love and it will bring you straight to Heaven's gate.

Maria Louise Wilson

Margot met and married an American soldier and moved to the United States.   She had five children. Her loving heart inspired those around her.

Ilse married a wonderful mild mannered man. They lived in Furth im Wald and had two boys.

Luise and Gerhard. She never got remarried. She and her son, Gunther, stayed in Furth im Wald.

Gunther at about age 16.   He later married a school teacher named Heidi. They had one son.

Maria and Ludwig Meier